IMPRISONED

'Jane Dudley?'

'Yes,' she replied.

'You must now come with me,' Bridges told her. He turned briskly about and began to leave the chamber. Jane followed him.

Behind her she heard boots rasp on the floor, and a gasp from Guilford. She wheeled around, and in panic saw that the guardsmen had restrained Guilford from following her.

'No,' she shouted. 'No!'

She felt Bridges seize her elbow and tug her towards the door. The guardsmen, likewise, had now pinioned Guilford's arms to his side. She shook her arm wildly, trying to free it.

'No, I will *not*. I refuse.'

One of the guardsmen detached himself and helped Bridges to drag Jane from the chamber.

'No!' her shout reached Guilford, as she disappeared.

'I will *not*.'

# *Lady Jane*

**A. C. H. SMITH**

From the screenplay by David Edgar

Now a major motion picture from Paramount Pictures

SPHERE BOOKS LIMITED
London and Sydney

First published in Great Britain by
Weidenfeld and Nicolson Ltd 1985


Published by Sphere Books Ltd
30-32 Gray's Inn Road, London WC1X 8JL

TRADE
MARK



Set in Times

Printed and bound in Great Britain by
Cox & Wyman Ltd, Reading

# I

In the Tower of London, John Dudley, Duke of Northumberland, was seated at a gilt-legged table, beside a log fire. He was waiting for the news from Tower Hill, which Sir John Gates would be bringing him. He had no doubt what the news would be, but these things had to be witnessed. While he waited he brooded on the line of succession to the throne. He took a sheet of parchment and began to sketch out the royal family tree.

After a while he paused, laid down his quill, and reflected on his work, slowly rolling his lower lip with his forefinger. Then he stood up and went to look out of the window of his office. Rain streaked the glass, and the bitter wind of a dark winter morning shook the bare, dripping branches of the trees outside. The courtyard and lawn below the window were empty. Soon enough, people would be coming back inside the walls of the Tower, from the hill to the north, from where the wind blew. Sir John Gates would be among them.

The Duke of Northumberland went back to his table and returned his attention to disposing of the throne.

On Tower Hill, Gates stood at the rear of the crowd below the scaffold, so that, while observing the demeanour of the Duke of Somerset, his eyes could also keep watch on how others were responding to the execution. It was two years since Somerset had been condemned to death. Were any here foolish enough to remember their disquiet at the verdict, and to give voice to it?

The man with the axe was a giant figure, dressed all in red, his face masked. 'Do you forgive me, my Lord?' he asked.

'I forgive you,' the Duke of Somerset replied, and he turned to address the crowd, their heads bared in the rain. 'Dear friends, I am brought here, as you know, to die. But I pray you,' – the Duke raised his voice above the shouts and growling – 'I pray you, make no noise, but keep yourselves quiet, for my sake.'

The people were reluctant to comply. They were here to see an execution, because that was what executions were for, but the Duke of Somerset was not a man they were glad to see die. His crime was supposed to be that he had treasonably plotted to have Privy Councillors murdered, so as to secure himself as Lord Protector of the Kingdom. Everyone there knew that the charge was absurd, and wickedly invented. Even so, some said, what if he had so plotted? England would be well rid of the villainous pack of Councillors, and most particularly of the Duke of Northumberland, who had succeeded as Protector. Somerset they knew to be a kindly man, one who would settle quarrels with reason rather than a blade. His loyalty to the boy-king had never been in doubt, nor had his care for the King's people, be they Catholic or reformed. It was well known that it had not been his wish to see rebellions cruelly put down. Men dispossessed of land and livelihood, and then told they must no longer say their prayers in the old Latin but in English, had rebelled, and been killed for it – but that had been the doing of overreaching Lords, in spite of Somerset. This man did not deserve to be on the scaffold on a raw, misty morning. They would tell him so, ere he died, even though he bade them to keep the peace. 'You are falsely accused, my Lord,' one shouted, and others roared their agreement.

The Duke continued, 'In my life I served my King with diligence' – he paused, while the people quietened – 'and now your duty is at one with mine: to pray for His Royal Majesty, and for his Church.'

The crowd was silent now. On the scaffold, attended by noblemen, priests, officers, and the headsman, the Duke drew a deeper breath for the final words he had to say, but still his voice faltered. 'May God grant the bounties of His wisdom to the man who takes my place.'

At that, a roar was fetched from every throat in the crowd. While Somerset quickly took off his doublet, embraced his friends, was blindfolded, and knelt at the block, those on the scaffold watched nervously as a riot surged towards them, apparently bent on rescuing the Duke. The guards at the foot of the steps levelled their halberds at the tumult of waving fists, glaring eyes, bellowing mouths. The crowd stopped a foot short of the halberds' points, but those behind threatened to impale the leaders with shoving and trampling. No one but himself heard the Duke's last words, as he spread his arms wide. 'Lord Jesus, save me.'

The falling axe ended the Duke's life and the riot simultaneously. Blood spurted from the decapitated torso. The headsman had done his job well, a clean cut through the neck, no maimed and writhing thing to be put out of its misery, as sometimes happened. The body was wrapped in sackcloth and taken for burial, the head to be impaled on Traitors' Gate, joining many others, some of them years old.

Behind the noisy crowd Sir John Gates had stood silent, watching. He was captain of the King's Guard. More important, he was a man whom the Duke of Northumberland trusted. There were not many. The business done with, he turned and made his way across the drawbridge back into the Tower, crossing the tidy lawns and courtyards, past turrets where damp flags flapped in the wind, gleaming cupolas, white stone battlements, to the room where Northumberland was waiting. 'It's done,' Gates told him.

'Did he die well?' Northumberland asked, without looking up from the table.

'Yes, he died well. The rabble did not behave well. They made some noise over it.'

Northumberland shrugged. The noise would not last long. It was the end of something, that noise, not the beginning: the end of an offence given five years ago, in 1547, when the dying Henry VIII had chosen a Protector. With only one son, and the boy but ten years of age, Henry had had no alternative, but it had been a grievous decision for him. A protectorate had always created dissension and unrest. Men and women yet alive remembered the last Protector, Richard, Duke of Gloucester, who had not been delicate in promoting himself to be King Richard III. Divisions in the kingdom were anathema to the Tudors. Religious heterodoxy had to be tolerated, if only to appease Spain; as Henry himself had remarked, he allowed the Bible to be 'disputed, rhymed, sung and jangled in every ale-house and tavern'. But political dissension, touching on the unity of the realm, the perfect circle of the crown, could only offend God and bring mischief and desolation.

For the period of Edward VI's minority, his father had chosen the boy-king's uncle, the Duke of Somerset, as Protector. Northumberland had been patient. While awaiting the ripe time to depose Somerset, he had given his attention to the young King. At first he had impressed Edward with his mastery at sports: Northumberland was an athlete, archer, horseman, at fifty years of age still the finest jouster in the land, and he could always spare time of an afternoon to join His Majesty at the butts and coach him in handling the longbow. Though a puritanical man in his private life, the Duke dressed handsomely, almost gaudily, and he exercised a jaunty charm over anyone he wished to cultivate. His sensual lips were ready to smile, his eyes to twinkle coldly. His hair was dark, but the beard and moustache were tinged with red. The King's youthful but high-minded devotion to the reformed religion, which was now being called Protestantism, found nothing but encouragement and approval in the Duke, who had brought up his own sons and daughters in the same creed. As Edward grew older, Northumberland flattered the boy by consulting him on all important decisions, and by insisting that His Majesty must attend all meetings of the Privy Council, to exercise the royal prerogative. Edward was not loath to do so. Since his earliest years he had been made to know how conscientious a Tudor King of England had to be, and his heart was keen to live up to his late father's expectations of him. One further bond between King and Duke was better not dwelt upon. Both had lost their fathers while still young boys. Northumberland's father had been executed within days of Edward's father's accession to the throne.

In due course Northumberland had judged that it was time to have done with the ineffectual Duke of Somerset. Having secured the verdict against him by buying sufficient testimony, Northumberland had told Somerset, in Westminster Hall, 'For myself, I willingly forgive you everything, and will use every exertion in my power that your life be spared.' For two years, at any rate. It had been necessary to keep Somerset in the Tower until the storm had blown over, not only for the sake of the common people but also because King Edward had been fond of his uncle.

Northumberland completed what he had been doing at the table, and turned the parchment round so that Gates could see it:

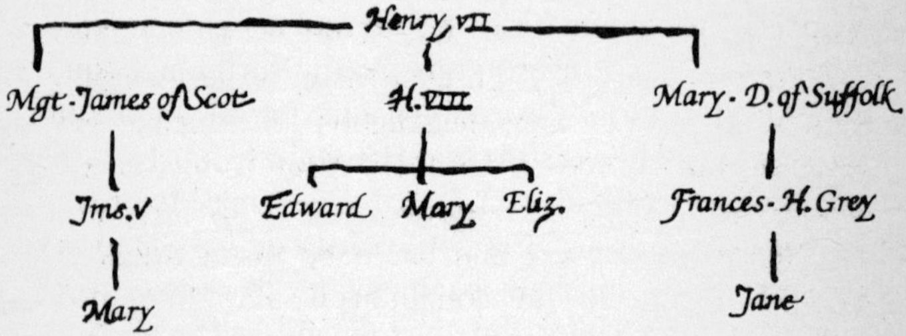

'My Lord?' Gates was frowning at the design.

Northumberland sighed, and smiled. 'In the last will of the King's late father, the succession is quite clearly lineated: the line of his elder sister, the Scottish line, or some might call it the French line, ruled out.' The Duke scratched out 'Mgt' and her heirs. 'So,' he continued, 'one: his son, King Edward. Two: his elder daughter, the Princess Mary. Three: his younger daughter, the Princess Elizabeth. Four: Frances of Suffolk, daughter of his younger sister. Five: her eldest daughter, the Lady Jane.' The Duke slowly ringed the name of Jane with his quill.

Gates, having thought he understood, was now frowning again. 'But surely, my Lord, the true prospect is that when King Edward shall marry and bear a son –'

'Exactly,' Northumberland interrupted. 'When the young King shall marry . . . The question is, shall marry whom?' He sat back in his chair, stroked his nose with the quill, and looked quizzically at Gates.

The Duke of Northumberland's idea that the young King should marry Lady Jane Grey was a political calculation on his part, an element in his strategy for tightening his own grip on the kingdom. In principle, His Majesty was betrothed to the French Princess Elisabeth, but that was an error unconscionably condoned by the fool Somerset, and could be disregarded. A French interest in the kingdom would annoy the Emperor Charles of Spain, upset the balance of power, and undermine Northumberland's sway. Far better for the boy to marry an English girl, of the reformed religion, from a family who would be ruled by Northumberland.

The same idea was cherished by Lady Jane's parents, but in their case the motive was simple ambition. Their family home, Bradgate Manor, stood confidently and comfortably in six miles of Leicestershire parkland. Unlike the old country seats, which had been fortified, the newly built Tudor mansions were designed for peace and elegant leisure. Behind the turreted gateway stood the great hall, flanked by wings to form a courtyard. An ornamental tower rose at each end of the hall. The whole of the manor-house was built in the pale red brick of the Midlands, faced with white stone and timber. The rooms were large and well lighted by latticed bay windows. The great hall could seat two hundred guests, at long tables below the dais where the Duke and Duchess of Suffolk dined with their family. As well as invited guests, any passing traveller was made welcome. The hall was encircled by galleries, and minstrels played on a balcony. In the family apartments carpets and tapestries were to be seen. That was what they were for: to be seen. The Suffolks desired to be in fashion, be it the fashion of costume, furnishing, intellect, or power.

Henry Grey, the Duke, was a capricious man, thought by no one to be formidable in anything. To his peers he was affable, to his children and inferiors he spoke testily as a rule. It was his wife Frances who wished to enhance the family's fortunes. Like her uncle, King Henry VIII, she had excelled at sports and dancing when young, but now the once healthily ruddy face had become rubicund, powdered flesh, enfolding narrow little eyes. Fourth in line to the throne, she had no expectation of succeeding her three younger cousins. What she did expect, and more than expect, was that the eldest of her three daughters would marry the King, who was exactly of an age with the Lady Jane. For that reason Jane had already spent years at Court, as a young girl, in waiting on Catherine Parr. The Duke of Somerset's younger brother, Thomas Seymour, had undertaken to make a royal match for Jane. Money had changed hands on account. To Frances's rage, nothing had yet come of it. Edward and Jane were friendly with each other, but friendship was irrelevant to marriage. No betrothal had been contracted. Now Seymour and Catherine Parr were dead, and Jane was living at home again. For the present, the best that could be done with her was to procure as good an education for her as any nobleman's son might expect.

The girl was apt. Truth, philosophical truth, above all the religious truth of the reformed religion, were her daily and abiding care. Her tutor, Aylmer, assured the Suffolks that Jane had a fine, enquiring, receptive mind. Well, that was something to recommend her. She had none of the family's robustness, being small-boned and fair in complexion. It was a pity that she was short, but a greater pity that, since being at Court, she had given proof of a robustness in spirit that she lacked in body. She had opinions and inclinations of her own, and was not ashamed to assert her independence of will even when it ran counter to what her parents knew was best.

It was not unusual, then, in the dying days of 1552, that Jane should be seated beside an alcoved window, reading, while her family were out hunting the red deer in the company of King Edward, Northumberland and two of his lusty sons, and Sir John Gates. The deer park extended all around the manor-house and was enclosed by a wooden paling fence against poachers and others who behaved as though the park were common land. When she heard the hounds give tongue, and the hunters, on their cumbrous, knightly horses, give halloo, Jane did no more than glance through the window. Immediately outside was a formal garden bordered by a brook. To one side was the tiltyard. Beyond, in the park, was a lake, clumps of trees, and a few scattered cottages which housed some of the family's three hundred servants. Rather than seek a glimpse of the hunt, Jane's gaze dwelt on the far horizon, where Chartley Forest was divided by valleys and dales. Soon her eyes would return to the book on her lap.

Up the long, tree-lined drive and into the courtyard of the manor-house came a coach and pair. It halted, and an elderly priest in a cassock stepped out. He stood for a while in hesitation, confused by the activity around him. Liveried servants were hastening in all directions with arms full of holly, ivy, kindling and sticks. Six men were hauling an enormous Yule log across the flagstones. Others were rolling a barrel towards the great hall. A steward stood in the middle of it all, apparently directing the traffic. At the side of the courtyard, a troop of the King's Guard had been stationed by Sir John Gates to keep watch.

The priest approached a servant who was carrying nothing and seemed to have a minute to spare. 'Excuse me –'

The servant shook his head, and found a reason to trot hurriedly away.

The priest tried again. 'Excuse me,' he said to a maid with floury hands, 'I am Dr Feckenham, I am sent by the

Princess Mary, and I have letters for the King –'

She would not stay to hear him out, but called over her shoulder, 'Out hunting'.

'And for my Lord the Duke of Suffolk –' Feckenham called angrily after her.

The maid went into the house, but Feckenham's cry had caught the attention of the steward, who paced slowly across to the priest.

Feckenham looked him up and down. 'See here,' he said, 'I am Dr Feckenham –'

The steward nodded knowingly. 'Yes,' he said, and pointedly added, 'Father. We don't see many of your kind here, you must understand.'

Feckenham frowned. 'My *kind?*'

'Well,' the Steward shrugged, 'my meaning is the Catholic kind. The people here are all reformed.'

Feckenham understood, and was calm. It was no surprise, of course. Everyone knew that the Suffolk family were reformed, else the King would hardly have been spending Christmas here. What was always disconcerting was the insolence and condescension you could meet. It was not so everywhere, nor did it have to be. Quietly, Feckenham asked the steward, 'Is there anyone in the house who can receive me?'

'This way, please,' said the steward, and led him through the busy courtyard, crossed by a white-aproned flight of maids with trays, and into the manor-house.

In the park Northumberland and the rest of the hunting party were standing back to allow the King, a healthy, athletic young man of fifteen years now, to close cautiously, sword drawn, on the mauled and exhausted deer.

Feckenham was shown into a long, low room, and the door was shut behind him. The steward had not announced him. At the other end of the room Lady Jane was still reading her book. The grey dress she wore was as sober as Feckenham's black habit. Beside her was a plate of small, spiced cakes, which she liked to nibble as she read. In the middle of the room a table had been covered with meats and pies, cakes and puddings, all set out in silver dishes and platters, against the return of the hunters.

Although they had not met before, Feckenham knew who the young woman must be. 'My Lady Jane?'

Jane looked up, irritated at the interruption.

'I am Dr Feckenham, ma'am. I am Confessor to the Princess Mary –'

'Yes, I know,' Jane said, reluctantly putting her book down and standing to receive her visitor. 'How do you do?'

Feckenham approached her, trying discreetly to make out what book it was that had so engrossed her. 'You are not out riding,' he remarked.

'No.' She saw where his eyes were flickering, picked up the book and handed it to him.

He looked at it, then at her. 'Plato,' he said, 'in Greek. Is it your own choice to be deciphering that when you might be at the hunt?'

'Entirely,' Jane said. 'All their sport is but a shadow to that pleasure I find in Plato.' She met Feckenham's eyes, and was pleased to read in them that he appreciated her esoteric joke.

'It is not easy to read in the Greek,' Feckenham observed.

'You think not?'

Now Feckenham smiled teasingly, sat down in the window seat, folded his hands in his lap and looked at her expectantly.

She relished the challenge, but kept a calm, indifferent expression on her face. Finding her place in the book, she began to translate the passage she had been reading. 'The soul takes flight to the world that is . . . unseen . . .' Her glance questioned Feckenham, who pursed his lips. 'Invisible,' Jane corrected herself, irritated to have made an error so soon. 'But there arriving,' she translated quickly, 'she is sure of bliss and forever dwells in paradise.' She snapped the book shut and looked up.

Feckenham was smiling gently at her. 'It is Mr Aylmer who teaches you, is it not? I know not whether the teacher or the pupil deserves the more praise.'

'His kind patience is one of the greatest benefits that ever God sent me,' she answered. 'My parents are so sharp and severe. Whatever I do in their presence, whether I speak or keep silence, sit, stand or go, eat or drink, be merry or sad, be sewing, playing, dancing or doing anything else, I must do it perfectly or be cruelly threatened, and presented sometimes with pinches and buffets, and other chastisements which I will not name for the honour I bear my parents, so without measure that I think myself in hell, till the time comes when I must go to Mr Aylmer again.'

It was Feckenham's turn to conceal his true feeling, which was astonishment. 'So,' he said, nodding, 'in Plato you have no doubt read of the death of Socrates, who was condemned for the spreading of pernicious doctrines of religion to corrupt the young. What conclusions do you draw?'

'That if one has strong beliefs one should be prepared to die for them.'

'You are young to speak of dying.'

She smiled, with the pleasure of knowing a good answer. 'It was Socrates who tells us that the real philosopher has reason to be of good cheer when he is about to die. "When I come to the end of my journey," he said, "I shall obtain that which has been the pursuit of my life." '

'Tell me, my Lady,' Feckenham asked, 'what things would you die for?'

Without hesitation Jane replied, 'I would die to free our people from the chains of bigotry and superstition.'

Feckenham laced his fingers together and rested his chin on them. 'And what superstitions do you have in mind?'

'Well, for an example, the notion that no one but the Pope of Rome may speak to God. That God may not speak to us directly but only through the mouths of priests. That a piece of bread may be transmuted into the body of Our Saviour.' She took a cake and bit into it, her eyes looking pointedly at Feckenham.

The priest paused. He was not offended by her zeal but, rather, moved by the youthful enthusiasm of her intellect. He met Protestant objectors to his faith every day; but it was seldom indeed that he met a mind like hers, as bright and hungry as an eagle's eye. At length he quietly continued the argument. 'Did Our Lord Jesus not say, at His last supper, "Take, eat, this is my body"?'

'Yes, indeed,' Jane replied. 'Also, He said, "I am the

vine, I am the door." Was He a vine, Father? A door?' Ironically, she genuflected to a small door near the window.

Feckenham shook his head mildly. 'Who has been teaching you to say such things?'

'Do you suppose me incapable of thinking of them myself?' She might have added that her faith had been sharpened this past year by a correspondence she maintained with learned Calvinists in Zürich, who were delighted to assist the spiritual growth of one whom they assumed would marry the King of England. But she let that pass. She wished to be judged for her own sake, not as the product of what her tutors had instilled in her.

'I am sorry,' said Feckenham, and he was. The rebuke had been just. Hearing loud voices approaching, he desisted from further argument because there was something he wanted to say to her. 'You are a most remarkable young lady. While we will disagree on many controversies, it is a privilege for me to converse with one whose love of learning shines as yours does.'

Jane's mouth opened, but for a moment she had no answer. The frank generosity of what Feckenham had said stripped away her brisk self-assurance, and brought tears to her eyes. 'It is', she said, 'my only pleasure, Dr Feckenham.'

Frances, Duchess of Suffolk, strode into the room, followed by John and Robert Dudley, tall sons of Northumberland, and by her husband. Feckenham saw Jane's lips tighten, and knew it was because she resented the invasion of the frail intimacy the two of them had created. These people had a way of entering and standing in a room as though any existing tenure was cancelled forthwith. They were lords of whatever space they found themselves occupying. If they could, they would enclose the globe.

'Jane,' Frances said, nettled that her daughter had not greeted her.

'Oh', Jane responded, 'Mother.'

Ignoring the priest, Frances went to the table, picked up a joint of goose, and began to eat it with the appetite of one who has enjoyed the fresh air and wishes to show the stay-at-homes what they have missed.

'How was the hunt?' Jane asked, hating all artificial conversations.

'Splendid,' Frances answered between mouthfuls, 'quite splendid, thank you, Jane.'

'Ah, Jane,' her father said, as if he had remembered once again what a feckless daughter he had, a disappointment, a failure, a waste of the time and money they had expended on her education and introduction at court, and all this because of the perverse will of the girl.

'Good morning, Father.'

'So there you are.'

'Yes,' Jane said. 'Father, this is –'

'You should have been with us.' He would go on twisting and knocking this child until she came into shape, and the tools he used were those that stir shame, guilt, fear, need. He knew that she understood all that as well as he did, saw herself as his adversary, and even stronger than the ambition he had for her was his bitter determination not to be bested by her. She knew so little of the world's ways, and it irked him that she could arrogantly fancy herself to be wiser than he was, and cleverer, on account of book learning. He was not against book learning, but where was the book that would tell its reader: What you have learned in my pages is of no use to you until you have gone out and tested it, tempered it in the world's flames.

'Now, Father,' Jane said, 'let me introduce Dr –'

'But of course,' Suffolk said, feeling his body clench with anger, 'to go out with your family, out riding, working up a sweat, well, that is altogether too base and brutish a morning for one of your kind, is it not?' He was holding a piece of ham on the bone, and had to make an effort to bite it casually.

Jane looked at him with blank eyes, as the maimed deer had looked at the man coming to kill it.

'Answer your father, Jane,' Frances ordered.

Jane's eyes closed, and so quietly that it was rather a prayer than an answer she murmured, 'Oh, Mother, please'. She felt trapped. It was easy and delightful to converse with anyone affectionate, even someone with contrary opinions, like Feckenham, and it was not difficult to speak with servants and common people where no emotions entered in; but she could not imagine how to answer, how to dwell there at all, when hostility sat in the place marked out for love. Plato spoke of the earthly love that normally existed between parents and children, but nor he, nor the Bible, nor any teacher she had, took account of the soul's desolation when it meets hatred and rancour in those of the same blood. For years, now, it had made her feel as though her own body was turning against itself. It was something unnatural, and the only response she had found to it was desperation.

Suffolk was using Feckenham as an excuse to talk out

loud. 'Now you might suppose, Father, that a first-born of the House of Suffolk would be giving consideration to her future, in her sixteenth year. So you might think, instead of poring all day over books, she could spend some of her time on studying those worldly things that might be useful to a husband, and to getting a husband.'

'Father,' Jane sighed, imploringly.

Suffolk's pate had started to colour. 'Don't you think so, tell me, Dr –'

'Henry!' It was Frances's deep voice that interrupted her husband. She and everyone else, save Suffolk, had seen the King enter the room.

It was probably not through affectation, but the fact was that Edward habitually, as now, struck a pose – feet planted apart, thumbs in his belt, head held levelly back – that uncannily recalled his father to those old enough to remember the late King. As yet his face more resembled that of his mother, Jane Seymour, but the body was Henry's in an adolescent. His tastes – for music, dancing, hunting, and reading – were also inherited from his father. He had shown some aptitude for mathematics, and in such applications of it as the declination of the compass needle was coached by Sebastian Cabot, the grand old navigator. When Jane had been at court, she and the King had been good friends at an early age. Both serious children, even then they had discussed and agreed about the reformed religion. Etiquette had required that, even going in to play a game of cards with him, she should curtsy three times, kneel when he addressed her and again on leaving his company, kiss his hand, and walk backwards from the room, curtsying again at the door. In all of that there had been, for both of them, the elements of a game, but it was a watched game, with courtiers in attendance, and moreover a game which they knew would be played throughout their grown-up lives. And so they played it solemnly, and to perfection. Now, at fifteen years of age, the game was more complex. Within the curtsy was a soul, and outside it was a young woman's body, and both these things had gathered more importance than the respecting of courtly formalities.

Edward advanced from the doorway, where he was flanked by the tall figures of Northumberland and Gates. He saw the book on the window seat and asked, 'What were you reading, cousin Jane?'

She couldn't answer, couldn't bring into focus all the colours of her social life together in that room, find words for them all to hear. Distressed, she gestured vaguely at the book. She hoped the King would not think her offhand.

He picked the book up. 'Plato,' he said, and nodded. He put it down again, leaving it open at the same place. 'Good morning, Dr Feckenham,' he said to the priest. 'Are you come with letters from my sister?'

Feckenham bowed.

Edward was walking towards the table, his appetite as fresh as anybody's. Where he walked, others parted to make way. To no one in general and everyone in particular he remarked, 'Her learning is an example to us all.'

Jane closed her eyes, and breathed deeply with relief. When she opened them again she saw Northumberland looking thoughtfully at her.

That afternoon, in midwinter sunshine, Edward asked

Jane to walk with him in the park. She was glad to go. It was the first time since their childhood that she had had the opportunity to talk with him alone. With them went her nine-year-old sister, Katherine, and with Katherine had to go her linen doll, its face, with rouged cheeks, bobbing on a floppy neck as the girl trotted along behind them. They were also necessarily accompanied, at a distance, by Sir John Gates and the armed men of the King's Guard.

'Are they always like that to you,' Edward asked, 'your mother and father?'

Jane made a little smile. 'Most of the time. Their wills are strong, but so is mine. They are offended by it. Or, rather, by what it is I will.'

'What is that?'

She shrugged, and looked at the waters of the stream by which they were strolling. 'My preoccupations for years now have been the life of the spirit, learning. I love learning, in books above all. It is as though the wise man who wrote a book is speaking directly to me, for my sake alone. I can say these things to you, as I can to Mr Aylmer and Dr Feckenham and to all people of that sort, but I cannot say them to my parents and hope to be understood aright.'

Edward was nodding as he walked.

'What interests me most', Jane continued, 'is to know from such as Plato how we may come to truth for ourselves.'

'Without benefit of clergy?'

'Yes.' She beamed at him for his quick understanding.

'And your parents do not respect that preoccupation in you?' Edward asked.

'It is of no interest whatever to them. They follow the

reformed religion with no more thought or question, no *wanting* to question, than if they still blindly obeyed the dicta of Rome. I did try to persuade my father to see that it behoves each one of us to consider well our individual soul, and to interrogate it closely every day, and every thought and deed, but I do not try any more. I save my breath for cooling broth. I have come to detest their way of life.'

'Their unthinking way, you mean?'

'Oh, everything. The gambling, the drinking. Extravagance. It is all a way to avoid thought.'

'Hmmm,' Edward said, pacing along with his hands behind his back. 'Yes, yes. My sister, Princess Mary, is extravagant.'

'Your sister, Princess Mary, is a Roman Catholic.'

'Indeed, yes.'

'And you ought to put a stop to it,' Jane said.

Edward stopped and looked sternly at her. She had infringed his majesty. She thought of curtsying to him, but realized that it would seem sarcastic, and so she did nothing.

Katherine took advantage of the pause in their walk to crouch down beside the stream, moisten a handkerchief, and wipe her doll's face with it. 'There now,' she said to the doll, 'there now, are you feeling better?'

Edward looked at Jane. 'Did you ever play with puppets,' he asked, 'when you were a small child?'

Jane smiled wryly, and shook her head.

Edward answered with a similar smile, and they were able to look each other in the eye again with a shared knowledge. 'I seem to have spent my whole life listening to sermons,' he said.

'Better now,' Katherine said to her doll.

Jane was still silent, but she was easy again with Edward. Both knew what they could have said to each other about the lives they had led, and both knew it did not have to be said.

Jane's eyes moved from Edward's face when a movement behind him caught her attention. Some hundred yards away a man was standing, watching them. Jane frowned. 'Who is that man?' she asked.

Edward turned to look. 'Sir John Gates,' he replied. 'He's –'

The King stopped talking quite suddenly, and from his throat came a series of little gasps. His face had turned a creamy colour, and there was sweat on his brow. He was swaying, and gasping for air, and Jane did not know what to do, until he swayed so far that he was falling down. Then she ran forward to catch him, and held him up at least long enough to save him from a heavy fall.

'Jane,' Edward was wheezing, 'oh, I, oh I feel quite dreadful, Jane, oh, please . . .'

He was heavy in her small arms, too heavy to bear up. 'Sir,' Jane said, frightened, 'oh, Edward, in God's name, what is the matter with you?' She just managed to let his body slump on the ground without bruising.

Gates had seen the incident and was running towards them. In her panic she wondered if the man was an enemy of the King and was now coming to finish him off. 'Please,' Jane begged Edward, or Providence, 'what do I do?'

Katherine had come to stand beside her, and was looking down with a serious face at the gasping boy. With her moistened handkerchief she leaned over him and wiped his feverish brow. It seemed to help. Edward calmed, and his eyes opened. He sighed, with a longer breath.

Gates reached them, calling, 'Your Grace!'

Edward managed a sort of sighing grin and said, 'It's all right now, Jane, Sir John.' He nodded. 'It is passing. I am recovered.' He was taking deep breaths of air. With a smile he looked up at Katherine, his nurse. 'Better now,' he said to her.

Katherine nodded soberly.

Edward got to his feet. 'I am recovered,' he repeated.

'What was it?' Jane was asking. 'What was the matter with you?' She was confused, anxious, and angry at her own incompetence.

'It has passed,' Edward said. He held her by the shoulder for a moment, to say that she must not fret.

'Did you faint? Was that it?'

He shook his head, smiling fondly at her. 'Come on, cousin Jane. We are out for a walk, that is all.'

She was still upset, angry with herself, that evening, when she was dressing for the Christmas Eve banquet. Mrs Ellen, a sharp-faced woman who had once been Jane's nurse and now waited upon her, held up a dress for approval. The gold and silver tissue was tight at the bodice but opened out into an enormous, bell-shaped skirt. The sleeves were slashed, and hung so low that they nearly reached the ground. With the dress she would wear gold-threaded cambric cuffs, and a fan-shaped head-dress of white lace.

'It's very pretty,' Mrs Ellen observed.

'No it isn't,' Jane answered. She shook her head, to the consternation of the maid who was brushing her long brown hair for her. 'It's lush, and gaudy.'

Mrs Ellen clicked her tongue. 'It is a handsome gift from your cousin Mary, my Lady. Look at the quality of it.' She ran her hand over the rich fabric, and turned the hem up at the bottom of the skirt to reveal the lining of sable fur. 'It is beautiful. You should be grateful.'

Jane dismissed the maid with the brush, and stood up. 'No I shouldn't,' she said irritably. 'The Princess Mary should seek out better ways of using her money. And I shall wear the black dress, if you please, Mrs Ellen.'

The nurse looked sadly at the dress. She had been looking forward to seeing her Lady wearing it. 'As my Lady wishes,' she said, and took the brilliant garment away. At the door she paused. Without fully turning round, she remarked, 'You know, my Lady, sometimes . . .'

'Yes?'

Mrs Ellen shook her head and said, 'No, it's nothing.'

While she waited for her black dress Jane watched her own dark eyes watch herself from the mirror. Hers was not a face made for laughing, she knew that. The shadowy rims of her lower eyelids made her appear slightly sombre, so that all her life she had had to bear with Mrs Ellen and other well-meaning souls who said, 'Be cheerful, my Lady. There's no cause to grieve.' That was still as true as it ever was, but tonight she thought she could read in her eyes a trace of the grief and guilt she had experienced that afternoon, when for a space of two minutes Edward had seemed mortally ill, and she had no idea at all of what she might do for him. She thought she would never forget the sudden, sweating pallor of his face – always hear that rasping for breath in his throat. She knew that one might awake healthy in the morning and be dead by nightfall of the plague, but such calamities did not befall kings, did they? Nor strike anyone dead within minutes.?

She heard a knock at the door in the outer room, followed by Mrs Ellen whispering to the caller. Coming hastily back into the dressing-room the nurse announced, in an urgent voice, 'My Lady, it is the Duke.'

Jane did not understand.

Raising her hands, Mrs Ellen made it plain. 'My Lord the Duke of Northumberland, my Lady. He is come here to speak with you, and is waiting in the anteroom for you.'

Jane refused to be impressed by so distinguished a visitor waiting upon her. 'I see. Well, then . . .' She gestured to the black velvet dress, with padded shoulders and white yoke and cuffs.

Helping her into it, Mrs Ellen felt she had to say what was on her mind. 'I love you deeply, my Lady,' she murmured. 'You are so intelligent, always were, and you will be beautiful, I'm sure of that, but sometimes, you are just . . .' She hesitated.

'I am just what, Mrs Ellen?'

'Impossible, my Lady.'

The tall, slim figure of Northumberland stood up as Mrs Ellen ushered Jane into the anteroom. The Duke bowed his head and kissed the small hand. Jane was wondering why Mrs Ellen had withdrawn, leaving her alone in this man's company.

'My Lady Jane,' Northumberland began, 'the King has sent me.'

'Yes, my Lord?'

'He was anxious to inform you that he is quite

recovered from the *malaise* that briefly afflicted him this afternoon, when he was walking with you.'

'Well,' Jane said, bewildered, 'I am glad to hear it, my Lord. Thank you for taking the trouble to come to tell me.'

Northumberland stood up at his full height, looking down at her. He saw that she had not understood his message at all. He continued: 'His Grace is so entirely restored to himself, praise be to God, that there is no need at all for you, or anyone else, even to mention that he suffered a moment of illness.'

'Ah.' She saw the point now. In a dry voice she said, 'I understand.'

'I am glad,' the Duke replied, and prepared to leave.

'You are asking me to lie.'

Northumberland answered instantly, 'I am asking you to refrain from volunteering information.' He paused, watching her unblinkingly.

She let her eyes elude his. Now she knew why Mrs Ellen had withdrawn. What she would have liked to ask this man, whom she had heard spoken of as the most powerful in England, was not, Why should I lie at your bidding?, nor even, What avails it that people should be ignorant of the King's *malaise*? It was not too hard to imagine the answers to both questions. No, what she would really have liked to know was, What ails the King? But she flickered a glance at those piercing eyes above her head, and knew that she would get no answer.

The Duke was saying, 'It cannot be too hard to understand for a young person with the learning to read Plato in the Greek tongue.'

Somewhere, on yellow strands washed by the Mediterranean Sea, where the hot sunlight beat down every day on rocks and sea and men alike, and the light was clear, nor were men's brains misted with imaginings and false desires, she supposed and hoped that the questions propounded by Plato were still debated, and the dialectic of reason held sway. England, this house, the steel trap of this man's gaze, imprisoned her. Reason was a private hobby.

Jane nodded. She understood.

Trumpets greeted the serving of each course at the Christmas banquet in the great hall. Cold cuts of ham and beef, mutton broth, stewed partridge, roast swan, and almond and honey cakes formed the first course. Every time meat was brought in, the line of servants doffed their caps in respect. Washed down with ale in earthenware mugs or wine in gilt goblets, the first course was followed by game soups, goose, cock pheasant, stuffed peacock, rabbit, venison, and egg fritters. Spoons, knives, bread and fingers served to convey it from dish to mouth.

On the dais, the King was splendid in purple silks, white fur and velvet, all set with rubies, pearls and diamonds. He was seated between Jane and Sir John Gates. Northumberland was next to Frances Suffolk, Henry with his daughter Katherine, and the two sons of Northumberland with their wives. Mrs Ellen and Dr Feckenham had also been invited to the top table for Christmas Eve. Below them the Leicestershire gentry, farmers, merchants and peasants made merry, six or seven score of them in all, frequently raising their mugs in grateful greetings to their hosts and masters.

Northumberland's thoughts, at that midwinter feast, were all for the King. While His Majesty lived, nothing was amiss. However, the Duke had to consider what would happen if Edward should succumb to the sickness he had. In that case his two sisters, Mary and Elizabeth, would have to be dealt with. The means would lie in their illegitimacy. Mary's mother, Catherine of Aragon, had been put aside, after more than twenty years, on the grounds of her prior marriage to Henry's brother. The mother of Elizabeth, Anne Boleyn, was technically not Henry's wife, even before her execution for treason, because the annulment of the first marriage had not been sanctioned. The shadow of bastardy over both women would serve to obscure them. Then this brutish Suffolk woman would have to be brought to renounce her own claim, so that the little Lady Jane could wear the crown, and be ruled by Northumberland. She could be married off to someone amenable. Northumberland's own unmarried son, Guilford, would be a safe choice. And then, handy-dandy, all would be well in Northumberland's realm.

While the King's health was in question, the Protector had to proceed with care. But on all counts it would be necessary to bring Frances Suffolk to heel.

'My Lady,' Northumberland said to her.

Frances belched. 'Yes?'

'Your daughter Jane is charming.'

'You find her so, my Lord?'

'Indeed. How old is she now?'

'Fifteen years.'

'And she has not been seen at Court.'

'She has been.' Frances drained her goblet. 'When Seymour . . .'

'Yes, yes, but I mean, not since she became a woman. She is remembered merely as the King's playmate.'

Frances snorted, and had her goblet filled again. Northumberland waved away the crystal jug from his own goblet.

'Well,' he continued, 'there you are. Fifteen. The same age as the King.'

Frances nodded. 'Born in the same month, October.'

Northumberland smiled, until she looked at him. Then he slowly shrugged. What could be more apt, his gesture said, what more could one ask?

Frances peered at him, thinking she knew his meaning, but not certain of it after so much feasting.

From the minstrels' gallery the trumpets brayed a fanfare for the next course. Servants streamed in with tureens of almond cream soup, covered dishes of fish, baked apples, bowls of nuts, syllabubs, creams, cakes, pastries, and puddings. More wine and beer flowed at all the tables. Some guests left to relieve themselves. Others broke wind at either end without leaving the table.

With a prance and rattle and beating of drums, the mummers capered into the hall, and began to act out their play in a space between the tables.

Open the door and let us in.
We trust your favour we shall win.
We'll do our best to please you all,
Each one of us, from short to tall:
And if you believe not what I say –
Enter the King of Egypt – clear the way!

Drum, tabor, rattle and sackbut made a cheerful noise as Prince George the dragon-slayer once again showed his mettle in combat with the infidel Turk.

'She's been well educated,' Frances said.

'That is very clear,' Northumberland answered.

Still not sure which cards she was supposed to be playing, Frances said, 'She can be wilful.'

Northumberland grunted. 'She'll grow out of that. You've had her brought up in the reformed religion?'

'Of course.'

The mummer prince was slain, and miraculously cured by a doctor of physick, and all was well, ending in marriage. Nothing was so amiss that it could not be amended by a little imagination.

Northumberland told Frances in a firm voice, 'I foresee a glittering future for your daughter, Madam.'

Frances nodded at him, with more emphasis than comprehension. At least, she thought, she would try to store it all away in her memory, and tomorrow perhaps she would be better able to plumb the deeper meanings of this disconcertingly sober man.

'So thus our talk is done,' said a mummer to the King, and his fellows came to join him in delivering the epilogue to Edward, and Jane seated next to him, pale in her black dress, but with a warmth in her smile after an evening in the company of one who seemed quite pleased that she should be as she was and did not wish her otherwise.

God bless you sir, afore your roaring fire.
God bless you mistress, in your fine attire.
None of this cheery house would we to chide,
An ye but bless us on this Christmastide.

The mummers bowed deeply. No one applauded yet. The King stood up, took a purse handed to him by Gates, stepped down and walked to the chief of the mummers, who bowed nearly to the floor. When the King bestowed the purse, everyone in the great hall clapped and stamped their applause.

As the mummers left, Suffolk signalled to the minstrels, who started up a pavane. The servants hurried around refilling the goblets and mugs. The King, still standing, held out his hand to Jane. Until the King would dance, no one else should.

Horribly self-conscious, Jane took the King's hand. He led her out into the open space vacated by the mummers, and with a pointing of toes, a stepping and swaying, they began the pavane, so beloved of the King's father. Stiff and nervous at first, Jane was gentled by Edward's fond smile for her, and she relaxed into the rhythm set by the musicians. Other couples came onto the floor, forming up into a paired procession behind each other.

Frances, with a goblet in her hand, stood watching with Northumberland. What it was to be a man, she was thinking. This King, these lords. 'I had two brothers,' she remarked. 'Died in the same week, of the sweating sickness. Had a son,' she grunted, 'didn't reach six months. Only girl children after that.' She glanced at Northumberland, who was watching the dancers. Frances shook her head enviously. 'Your handsome sons. Their lovely wives.'

'Yes,' Northumberland said, slightly wistful for some reason she could not fathom. 'My third son, Guilford, is not here with us.'

'They must be such a joy to you,' Frances said. 'Such fine, upstanding sons.' When Northumberland did not answer, Frances turned and walked slowly away, swaying slightly, as the dancers were.

She had gone before Northumberland sighed.

Guilford Dudley, who was not with his family at the

Bradgate Manor house-party, could at that moment have been seen screaming 'Kill!' at a cockerel daubed with white paint and crested with a mock triple crown of thick parchment. This was 'the Pope'. His opponent, 'the King', had been painted red and blue, and crowned with an equally crude coronet. The man who was accepting wagers in the cockpit had made the Pope favourite, but the other bird was having the better of the fight. Feathers flew and blood dribbled down where the blades tied to the cocks' feet slashed. Men's faces, red in the torchlight, bellowed their fancies on, and ribbed their neighbours who had wagered on the wrong one. 'Get in there, get in there!' Guilford muttered, clenching his fists, and when the Pope did flurry an assault he shrieked 'Kill! Kill him!' His handsome, square jaw was flaccid with drink and excitement. His companions, Thomas and Richard, exchanged a look behind Guilford's back. Their noble friend was in more extreme disarray than ever tonight. No paragons themselves, they found a peculiar pleasure in his company at times like this, which they would have been ashamed to recognize. Guilford at seventeen years of age was tall, straight-backed, pale in complexion, fair-haired and blue-eyed, the son of the most powerful man in England, and of a mother who doted upon him especially, perhaps because he resembled his father less than his brothers did. To see this scion slide deeper into dissolution, as the months passed, was unaccountably thrilling to them. Good fellows with him both, they professed a companionable concern for his increasingly wild ways, and it was Thomas and Richard who would pick him up at the end of an evening in the stews, and get him to a couch somewhere, to sleep it off, and start again the next afternoon.

'Come on, Clement! Go for him, Henry. Rip his legs off!' the jostling spectators shouted. 'Have at him, Pope! Up, up, King Hal!' The birds were exhausted now. They circled each other with heads held low, eyes still gleaming viciously. The blind instinct of the male tolerating no rival on his territory was all that drove them on, to the delight of the gamblers and the bookmaker, who adjusted his odds to attract late money. 'A shilling I'll lay to four of yours on the King. A shilling to your shilling about the Pope.' More wagers were quickly made, more urgent appeals were hollered. 'In there, Your Holiness, get in. Go for the eyes, the eyes! Now you have him, Your Majesty. Hack, hack!'

Guilford, crouched forward and staring intensely, was chanting, 'Kill, kill, damn you! Rip him open! Blind him and rip him and kill!'

His friends nodded at each other and took Guilford by the arms. 'Now, come on, Guilford. Let's away.'

Incensed, he threw them off, and glared at them, wiping his mouth. 'Wha'? Wha' you mean?'

'Come, now,' Richard said, 'my Lord. It is time to go.'

'*Go?*' Guilford shook his head violently, which caused him to stumble and fall on one elbow. From there, he rolled over in the dust, and screamed, 'Tear his plaguey legs off, damn you, Pope!' He looked up at Thomas with a forlorn smile. 'I've a shilling on His . . .' – he hiccoughed, shook his head, and tried again – 'on the Pope, Thomas. You don't know that, do you?' He lay flat on his back, and shook with laughter.

Triumphant cheers opened his eyes again, and he

lurched, blinking, towards the cocks. The Pope had only one good leg left, and was hobbling in little circles trying to fend off the flying, two-legged assaults of Bluff King Hal. Guilford stared for a while, then muttered, 'God's teeth'. He shook his head, as though to rearrange the evidence of his eyes. The Pope had lost his crown, and had surrendered the contest and his life. He lay on his side, eyes open, unable to defend himself at all against the incessant, furious attack of the other.

Still shaking his head, Guilford suffered himself to be led away.

'A merry Christmas,' Richard said to him, with a wry smile at Thomas.

The mummers had eaten supper in the kitchen and were in a hallway at the back of the manor-house, eagerly counting out the assorted coins in the purse bestowed upon them for their performance. It was disappointing. In their grandfathers' time, six shillings and eightpence would have been a handsome reward. Now, in currency debased to pay for the late King's struggles with France and Scotland, it bought sniffs and wrinkled noses. One of the mummers picked up a small shilling piece, more copper in colour than silver, and regarded it with scorn. He tossed it to one of the villagers gathered at the doorway from the house. The villager held it in the palm of his hand and blew on it, as though it would float from him. 'Time was', he said, 'a shilling really was a shilling. Our mint's a counterfeit.'

'It is better to trade in kind,' said the mummer. 'I barter my cheese for what I take from the ale-house.'

The villager laughed. 'Unless the keeper can get

himself glorious on your cheese, John, I wonder he consents to the trade.'

In the great hall the minstrels were playing for just a small party of late revellers, most of them young. Northumberland stood watching his sons and their wives break from a pavane into a brisk galliard. It was nearly midnight. He left the hall and strolled along a gallery leading to his bedchamber for the night.

At a window he paused. Across the courtyard, at another window, he could see Edward and Jane together. They were looking down at a torchlit procession of waits crossing the courtyard, singing in the first moments of Christmas Day.

Nowell sing we, both all and some,
Now Rex pacificus is y-come.
Exortum est in love and lysse.
Now Christ his gree he gan us gysse,
And with his body us brought to bliss,
Both all and some, both all and some.

De fructu ventris of Mary bright,
Both God and man in her alight,
Out of disease he did us dight:
Both all and some, both all and some.

Northumberland could see that both the faces at the window wore wistful expressions. Were they touched by this ancient rite? He doubted it. More likely they were reminded of their own simplicity in times past. 'Put away childish things,' Northumberland murmured to himself. 'For now we see through a glass, darkly.'

Both Edward and Jane jumped when a voice spoke

softly behind them. It was Dr Feckenham. 'Et ecce angelus domini stetit –'

Edward held his head back, and looked down his nose at Feckenham. 'In our own tongue, I pray you, doctor.'

Feckenham did not hesitate. With an amicable smile, he translated. 'And lo, the angel of the Lord came upon them, and said unto them, Fear not, for behold – I bring you good tidings of great joy, which shall be to everyone.'

Such charming goodness emanated from this priest that it was impossible for the King not to feel contrite at his own admonishing words, however sincere they had been. He smiled back at Feckenham, and came close to a slight bow of his head.

Feckenham looked from one to the other, and said, 'A merry Christmas to your Grace, and to you, my Lady.' With a slow bow, he withdrew, and walked away along the corridor. Northumberland was slowly approaching. Feckenham bowed, and the Duke inclined his head in acknowledgement.

The waits were leaving the courtyard, singing the last verse and burden of their carol.

Gloria tibi, ay, and bliss,
God unto his grace he us wysse,
The rent of heaven that we not miss:
Nowell sing we, both all and some,
Now Rex pacificus is y-come.

Edward took Jane's hands in his, for their old friendship, and whispered, 'And straightway there was with the angel a multitude of the heavenly host . . .'

'Lauding God and saying . . .' Jane responded.

'Glory to God on high, and on earth . . .'

'Peace. Goodwill to all men.'

'A merry Christmas, Lady Jane.'

She smiled brightly, and squeezed his hands.

From where Northumberland stood watching, a distance away, it might have been a pair of lovers, their eyes shining for each other. Well, he thought, no harm in it if they were. It would be easier, then, to arrange their marriage, supposing that the King's health mended. And let them, for the present, go on believing that 'Goodwill', spoken with bright eyes and holding hands, was a real force at work in the world. Even at their age, he did not remember believing that himself, but perhaps he had . . . perhaps he had. 'When I was a child, I spake as a child, I understood as a child, I thought as a child: but when I became a man, I put away childish things.'

Some weeks later Jane was at Princess Mary's house, in Essex. After the excitements of Christmas she had been poorly, and a change of air was thought advisable. The opportunity arose when Mary sent to invite her cousin to stay with her. She was having her portrait painted, Mary wrote, and while the artist was there she would like to have him paint little Jane's portrait, too.

Jane waited on an alcoved seat in the entrance hall until she was fetched by Lady Anne Wharton, Mary's attendant. 'The Princess Mary is free to see you now,' said Lady Anne, primly. 'Would you follow me, please?'

As she led Jane along a gallery, Lady Anne explained, 'She asks me to apologize for keeping you waiting, my Lady. She was finishing a hand of trump. Do you play cards?'

'No,' Jane answered. 'No, I don't.'

'You're wise,' Anne said, with a little sideways smile. 'She's very good.'

Jane did not respond.

At one side of the gallery they passed a small shrine. The light of thirty candles glinted on gilt and silver chalices, dishes, and other vessels, and illuminated a painted Madonna and Child. The altar was covered with a richly embroidered cloth, on which stood a large crucifix of silver. Before it, on a small dish, was the Host.

Anne bobbed a curtsy as they walked past the shrine.

Jane had glanced in horror at the display, seeing a panoply of superstition where there should have been a bare, empty space for faith to enter in and truth to recognize itself. God was to be served at a simple table, not a sacrificial altar. To worship Him, the body had need of pure air, not this vulgar fume of incense that she could feel sullying her skin. And the sacrament was celebrated in ordinary bread, and if any were left over it was given to the curate to eat for his breakfast. She could not contain her disgust, nor saw any reason to do so. 'Why do you curtsy?' she asked. 'Is the Princess Mary within the chapel?'

'No, my Lady,' Anne replied. 'I make my curtsy to the Host, to Him that made us all.'

Jane stood and looked at the wafer of bread. It was no more than cannibalism, this Popish dogma of transubstantiation, no better, if believed in, than the sacrifices practised by poor heathens beyond the ocean seas. Was Christ to be tormented again by having His precious Body rent and torn by the teeth of Christian people? 'Why,' Jane said, 'how can He be there that made us all, and the baker made Him?'

A deep voice behind her said, 'Well, can this be my little cousin Jane?'

The two girls turned around sharply. Anne hurriedly curtsied to the Princess. So did Jane, because of her courtly training rather than her will. 'Oh, Ma'am,' was all she said.

Mary was short, like Jane, but at thirty-seven had none of her cousin's graceful slightness. Where Jane preferred a simple dress, Mary wore satins and velvets of several colours, and at the face, neck, and hands was adorned with jewels and gold. Her nose and chin were pointed, and if she had ever had Jane's white, sharp teeth they had been ravaged by time and feasts. For the younger woman, truth was the highest ideal, to be pursued whatever it cost. Mary had learned the Tudor art of compromise. Without it, she could scarcely have survived five stepmothers and repudiation by her father. One thing she never forgave him, never accepted as compromise: his forcing her, with threats, to acknowledge his supremacy over the Church. She trusted in God to show her the way she should follow on earth in order to expiate the sin she had committed then.

She stepped forward and genuflected to the Host, then turned back to Jane, taking out a pair of eye-glasses to examine her cousin. 'Now let me look at you,' she said. 'Well, well-a-day, how you've grown. Not tall but into a woman.' She laughed. 'It is definitely time you were preserved in paint. I am delighted to have arranged it for you.' And it was true, she was delighted. Her impulsive and affectionate nature took pleasure in bestowing gifts and surprises on those near to her. If this little cousin Jane was growing up to be a fanatic, so much the worse for her; but Mary would wait to see whether it was truly Jane, or her tutors speaking through her young mouth, who had mocked the Host of the Lord. Putting her glasses away, she held her arms out. Embracing Jane, she whispered in her ear, 'If I were you, I should take more care, little cousin.'

Mary led the way to a high-ceilinged drawing-room, which was serving as a studio for the painter. The Princess's portrait was virtually finished. It stood on an easel, and beside it was a dummy, dressed as Mary was in her portrait, in purple satin. The forearms of the dress were slashed and rich with lace, the collar folded back to reveal a lining of silk and the ruffed neck of her chemise. Below the ruff hung a necklace of silver and hundreds of diamonds. A larger necklace, of white pearls, lay on her breast, with a pendant in which an enormous ruby was set in gold studded with smaller rubies, pearls, and an opal. More rubies adorned her ears, and the deep-brown velvet head-dress, drawn up at each side to form a triangle with her chin, was outlined with pearls and sapphires.

'Have you worn the dress I sent you as a gift for Christmas?' Mary asked.

Looking at the dressed dummy and the portrait, remembering the stifling superstition of the shrine and the ostentation of the dress Mary had sent her, Jane hesitated. She wanted to tell the truth, but the truth was that she had rather go naked than defile God's nature with wanton, voluptuous trickery. 'I have not worn it yet,' she answered.

'It might have proved suitable for this portrait,' Mary said, looking studiedly at the simply dressed, fresh-faced child beside her.

The painter was standing beside a new, whited board. With a bow he motioned Jane to stand nearer the light of the high windows. She did as he bade her, and almost instinctively assumed the same pose as Mary had in her portrait, straight and four-square, the hands clasped in front, the head held serenely high and assured.

Mary noticed the similarity. Her eyes moved between the picture of herself, the extravagent apparel, the crabbed face, and time's parody, the young Lady Jane. To the painter she said, 'Master Gwillim, do try to make the face this time look a little less – morose.'

The painter bowed again, as Mary swept out, followed by Anne.

If Jane heard the envy and pathos of the remark, she gave no sign. She remained drawn up in her pose, another Tudor noblewoman, confident of her status and her purpose.

The Duke of Northumberland was at Whitehall Palace. Outside the window he could see his son, John, at the archery butts with King Edward. Northumberland had taught both of them all they knew about the handling of a bow. The room where he stood was the one in which the King's physician, Dr Owen, ground his herbs and roots, mixed his balsams, distilled his essences, compounded his specifics, and prepared his poultices. Dr Owen was seated. The expression on his face was grave.

'How long?' Northumberland asked.

'The autumn.' Owen shrugged. 'Possibly.'

'Possibly that early, or possibly that late?'

'That late,' Owen said glumly.

Northumberland went on watching the arrows thud into the targets. Eventually he asked, 'Do you think he knows?'

Owen shrugged again, as physicians do, seeing so

much of first and final causes and knowing how useless logic is in seeking to connect them.

Northumberland left the room and walked, deep in thought, to the butts. It was his impression that Edward did know he was dying. On the secret visits that the Duke made to him at night, the better to advise the young King discreetly, Edward had lately been more disposed than ever to repose all his confidence in Northumberland. The Protestant cause, enrichment of the coinage, trade and exploration through the agency of the Merchants Adventurers – all these projects, on which Edward had filled pages of his private notebooks, were now wholly entrusted to the Duke. That was the behaviour of a young man who either had lost his interest in ruling the kingdom, which was inconceivable in Edward's case, or lost his expectation of it. Northumberland had also assumed control of the kingdom's finances, which was necessary if he were to govern all else. To reward himself for shouldering far more responsibility than the previous Protector, he had annexed the lands of the archbishopric of Durham for his own. He knew that he was hated, and called a dictator. That cost him no sleep. His responsibilities did.

Each time Edward loosed an arrow, attendants came forward to put a cloak and furs about him. He was glad of them in the treacherous sunshine of March.

'You ought not to remain here much longer, your Grace,' Northumberland said. 'It is cold. And you have ambassadors to see.'

The King grinned wistfully, nodded, and handed his bow to John Dudley. 'I saw some children near Blackfriars yesterday,' he said to Northumberland, while the attendants helped him on with a greatcoat trimmed with sable. 'They were playing with a kind of puppet, but it had strings knotted to the limbs, which were attached to a bar held above the device. When they pulled or agitated the strings, the puppet was caused to dance in the merriest way.'

Northumberland smiled. 'Yes, it is an invention of the French. They call it a marionette.'

'I'd like one, please,' Edward replied. 'What did my physician say to you?'

Northumberland paused before answering. His eyes twinkled to hear His Majesty asking for a toy. 'How did you know that I have been with Dr Owen?' he asked.

Edward tapped his temples with his forefingers. 'My eyes are still effective, my Lord, even if some other parts of me leave something to be desired, I imagine.'

'Dr Owen says that we should all continue to be mindful of your health, sire.'

'That is a politician's answer,' the King said.

'I am a politician, your Grace,' Northumberland smiled.

Edward looked back at him with a knowing smile of such charm that, for a moment, Northumberland minded for the boy's sake, not the realm's, that the King was approaching death. Dr Owen had diagnosed consumption, and Northumberland had seen it before, this stark, intense beauty on the face of consumptives, as though it were a disease with the strange power of distilling and manifesting all that is best in the character.

When Edward left, with his attendants, John Dudley asked his father, 'How ill is he really?'

Northumberland ignored the question. Instead, he turned to John and asked him, 'Where is your brother?'

'Robert?'

'No,' Northumberland said impatiently, 'I know where Robert is. He is carving for His Majesty.'

John stroked his chin. 'Oh well, as for Guilford, sir, I should expect him to be about his studies. Otherwise you might well find him at his prayers.'

Northumberland grunted. '*You* are a politician.' He strode away. There was much to do, in consequence of Dr Owen's opinion.

Guilford Dudley was standing in a tavern in Eastcheap. He would not have been on his feet but for Thomas and Richard, who supported him, one each side, as though they were figures in a coat of arms.

The taverner had had enough of it. 'I – want – him – out,' he repeated dogmatically to Thomas and Richard, knowing that Guilford's ears had no more hearing in them than the handles of a jug.

He was wrong. 'And – what – I – want', Guilford giggled, 'issomemorewine.' He called loudly, 'Richard!'

'No more wine,' Richard told him, at his elbow.

'No more wine?' Guilford exclaimed. 'In a tavern? Have we drunk it all?'

The taverner announced, 'I am going to count to ten.'

'Bravo!' Guilford replied. 'It is not every night one meets an educated man in your position, sirrah.'

'No, sir,' the taverner answered, looking down at Guilford, who was virtually genuflecting to him, 'and I could say likewise about yourself. One.'

'It's bedtime, Guilford,' Thomas told him.

'Two.'

Guilford was making a valiant effort to stand up straight, since he wanted to say something dignified. 'Are you aware . . .' he began.

'Three.'

'. . . that you are addressing the most beloved son – well, as far as my mother . . .'

'Four.'

'. . . the most beloved son of the most powerful, important and foul-tempered nobleman in all of . . .'

'I know who you are, my Lord. That makes eight.'

Richard and Thomas were tugging hard at Guilford's arms, but he was bent on finishing his little speech. 'You see, my man, I do feel that . . .'

'Nine,' the taverner said.

Richard and Thomas exchanged a look and decided to leave their friend to his fate. They let go of his arms and went out into the street.

'Before you do anything precip – preciti –,' they heard him admonish the taverner, 'anything hasty, you ought to understand . . .'

But the taverner was not an understanding man. Guilford's body was flung from the tavern door as though onto a passing plague-cart. He landed on the cobblestones in a heap.

Bending over him, Richard and Thomas heard him say, '. . . with whom it is you deal', before his eyes closed. They looked resignedly at each other. Another load to carry tonight.

At the Suffolks' London home, Dorset Place, the calm, composed face of Lady Jane looked out from her portrait across a small hall. Standing before it, and admiring it, was Northumberland. He scratched his scraggy ginger beard, flecked with grey, and pursed his lips. 'She's a Tudor,' he observed.

'So am I,' answered Frances, with her mouth full. She

was seated behind him, at a table with cold meats, roast venison, onions pickled in cloves, and baked fruits. 'Try the brawn,' she offered. 'It's very good with onions.'

'No, thank you. I am not hungry.'

'It seems to me that you are growing thin with care. You should eat more.'

'Hmm,' Northumberland said, and drummed his fingers behind his back.

Frances wiped her mouth. 'So, John Dudley. Why have you come to see me? I am sure you have a mission.'

Northumberland turned, as though on a cue, and looked gravely at her. 'Madam, have you considered yet the matter of what is to become of your daughter Lady Jane?'

Frances realized that something serious was afoot, and she answered carefully. 'Yes, you know I have.'

'In that case, may I ask –'

She interrupted him. 'I can see no reason why she should not marry Edward.'

'I can,' Northumberland said.

Frances stiffened. This was not what she had expected, not what, she was sure of it, the Duke had been hinting at all these months. Some shift in his policy had occurred. 'What reason is there, then, my Lord?' she asked coldly.

'He's dying.'

Now her body went limp, all the wind gone from her sails. 'What?' Everyone knew that the King had not been in good health, and had been attacked by the measles or something and taken a long time to recover. But after his father's reign of nigh on forty years, it was shocking to hear that the boy was dying at sixteen years of age.

'He will be dead in – who knows, a month?' Northumberland said.

'God rest his soul,' Frances sighed.

'Indeed.'

Aware that Northumberland was continuing to look at her, Frances started to guess the nature of his mission. She looked up. 'What will happen then?'

From his pocket the Duke took a sheet of paper and laid it on the table in front of her, beside the half-eaten plateful of food. It was the chart of succession to the throne that he had shown Gates months before, though he had made a fresh copy of it, without the scratchings and ringings he had added then. 'Madam,' he declared, 'there will not be another Roman Catholic on the English throne.'

Frances spread her hands. 'The country people would not agree. They still adhere. I have been told so, often. Our reformed creed is found wanting. They are still attached to their Latin litanies and mysteries perfumed with incense. They pine for ornaments and precious baubles to assist their worship.'

'Of course they do,' Northumberland answered, 'as all pine for the things of their childhood. Many can remember the time before King Henry closed the canting monasteries, when every church was festooned with such baubles, on the altars, hanging from the walls.' He paused, and let his eyes travel from Frances's to the gold plate on the table, the candlesticks, the tapestries, and back to the jewellery at her neck. 'Of course they pine for what is no longer theirs.' He leaned forward, resting his knuckles on the table, and spoke with great intensity. 'And that, madam, is why, for you and, yes, for me as well, there *must* not be another of the Roman

Catholic persuasion on the throne of England. It cannot be.'

Frances was nervous. This man's eyes were so piercing when he chose to turn them upon you. To avoid them, she looked down at the paper he had placed before her, and began to interpret it. 'Um,' she muttered, tracing the family tree with a finger, 'if Edward dies leaving no heir –' She glanced up. 'And that is a certainty?'

'Yes.'

'Ah.' Frances looked down at the paper again.

'Then Mary is Queen . . .' Northumberland said, as though he were a tutor guiding his pupil through a Greek translation.

Frances understood. 'But Mary's mother was divorced. And she was declared a bastard.'

'Quite.' The Duke smiled encouragingly at her.

Frances looked at the paper, though she had no need to now. 'And the next in line is the Princess Elizabeth . . .'

'Whose mother Anne Boleyn was beheaded for her treasonable adultery with her brother.'

'Among others,' Frances added.

Northumberland took the knife from Frances's plate. He scored it across the names of Mary and Elizabeth, leaving gravy on the paper. Then he slowly drew the point under the name of Frances Grey, Duchess of Suffolk.

Frances's mouth was open, but she could find nothing to say.

'And so, behold,' Northumberland continued, 'the next in line to the throne becomes, my Lady . . .'

She was breathing heavily.

'. . . Frances of Suffolk.' He had not done with the

knife. He scored a ring around the name of Jane. 'Who could of course relinquish all her dues and rights in favour of her eldest daughter, the Lady Jane Grey.'

Frances sat up straight. She turned and examined Northumberland's face, her eyes narrow. 'Now why should I do *so*?' she asked slowly.

Before Northumberland could answer, Henry Suffolk clumped into the hall, in muddy boots. Hauling him were two great hounds, on leashes. They strained to reach the meat on the table. 'Ah, Frances, there you are,' Suffolk said, always breezy. 'Down, damn you, Jupiter!' The dogs were near to taking him off his feet. Struggling to control them, he went to the table to fetch something for them, and was surprised to see his wife still engaged on the meal she had begun before he took the dogs out. Taking a couple of bones from her plate, he dropped them down on the floor. 'Now down, do you hear me, Brutus? Down, both of you.' The dogs seized a bone apiece, and Suffolk had time to remark, 'Good Lord, Frances, are you still eating?'

'I was talking with my Lord Northumberland.' She spoke acidly. What right had Suffolk to reproach her for her appetite, when he had not the manners even to acknowledge their guest's presence in the room?

'Ah,' Suffolk said. He had been so occupied with the dogs that he simply had not had time to recognize Northumberland. 'Good evening, John.'

'My Lord.' Northumberland inclined his head.

'And what we were talking of,' Frances continued, 'was Jane's marriage, a subject which might be of more interest to you than your dogs, Henry. We were agreeing that it might become a matter of peculiar importance in the event of circumstances which – well, might arise.'

Suffolk nodded, understanding scarcely a word of what his wife told him, but sensing that a nod would be the most acceptable response at this stage.

Frances was speaking for Northumberland's benefit. She had got the point. 'In fact,' she continued, turning to him, 'I suspect that my Lord has somebody in mind for Jane.'

'Has he?' Suffolk was taken aback. Like his wife, he had until this evening supposed that Jane was destined for King Edward. But that could no longer be the case, else Frances would not be speaking as archly as she was, because it had been no secret to anyone in this house. This damned Northumberland, always arranging people's lives for them to suit his own stratagems. Suffolk, too, had once thought how agreeable it might prove to be powerful in politics; but when he saw the new men, like Northumberland, at close quarters, he no longer had the heart for it. The habits and pleasures of the old families – those were his ways, and he was too set in them now to change, or even to want to change if it meant the calculating heart, the merciless eye, of a man like this. Frances would have her way, he accepted that, but he would let it be known that the choice of husband for his eldest daughter was a question on which he had opinions to express. Sitting down now, with the dogs at his feet, he put on a haughty look for Northumberland. 'Perhaps', Suffolk said, 'my Lord will be good enough to let us know whom he has in mind.'

Effortlessly Northumberland moved into the role of suppliant, the lesser aristocrat proposing an alliance to the greater. 'My Lord,' he said, 'I believe you have not met my younger son Guilford, who is as yet unmarried. He is a quiet and studious boy, which is the reason why he has not been seen much in society. Even now, in fact, I imagine that he will be among his books, or else at prayer.'

All tastes were accommodated at the sign of the Flowering May Tree in Southwark. Whores buxom or boyish, short, tall, fair, dark, or auburn, with curly hair or straight, young girls or matronly women, of merry or melancholy disposition, some of them would leer at you lewdly, others affected a demure reserve. Whatever lickerish dream a man had, he could purchase it here for eight pence, four of which went to the whore, and four to Lucas d'Avray. Behind the front door of the brothel was a huge room that had once been a courtyard but was now roofed over, floored with wooden blocks, and carpeted. All around the walls the whores sat on benches. A client coming in would be mobbed by them. When he had chosen one of them, or more, they would sit together on the benches for a while, being entertained. In the centre of the room the unoccupied whores took turns to dance, in groups of four or six. An ensemble of three minstrels sat in a sort of box, slightly raised above floor level, which had once housed a horse. Ale, beer, wine and brandy were served throughout the house, for cash. The whores, also, had to be paid the eight pence in cash, at the outset. It was then their task to satisfy or exhaust the client as soon as possible, so that they were available for another. A clerk sat on the far side of the assembly, beside a door leading to the rooms with couches and beds, and he made a mark against a whore's name every time she went past him with a fresh client. Thus d'Avray kept his accounts. With the exception of whores who cheated, or clients who required boys no one was barred and everything was permitted in his house – and at some time or another everything occurred, human desires being various. The class of clients, too, was as diverse as could be imagined among those who had eightpence to spend.

Towards eleven o'clock on the evening when Northumberland had spoken to Frances and Henry Suffolk about his son Guilford, a lean, clean-shaven man walked along the street until he came to the door into d'Avray's house of pleasure. The man was one who had also been on the fringe of the crowd at the cockpit, a passer-by when Guilford was thrown from the tavern, and in general an observer, paid by Northumberland, of Guilford Dudley's habits.

At d'Avray's door he pointed, and stood aside. A gang of armed and booted men, who had been following him, rushed through the door. At a more leisurely pace Sir John Gates entered after them.

Whores were screaming and spitting at the armed men, who bundled them aside in their haste to examine each of the clients seated there. The uproar brought d'Avray into the room, wiping his mouth. 'What is this?' he demanded. 'Who are you? What do you want?' Ignored, he addressed himself to Gates, who was clearly in charge of the intruders. 'Who are you? Who has sent you here? Tell me what you want, and I will give it to you.' Gates ignored him likewise.

The armed men had examined all the clients in the first room, without finding what they were after, and had dashed past the clerk into the next room. Here, a dozen or so couches were to be seen, all within a common, unenclosed space. Most of them were occupied by a whore and her client, at various stages of their business.

One wretched fellow was howling in agony, his whore's teeth having closed upon him in her shock at the invasion. Among the clients were Richard and Thomas, Guilford's friends. Thomas, being more or less fully clothed still, made for the door into the interior room, but was intercepted by one of the armed men. 'Where is he?'

'Who?' Thomas had recognized Gates in the doorway, and guessed what was up. But he himself, Thomas reckoned, would not be known to the armed man.

A knee in his groin persuaded him he was wrong about that. Thomas gestured at the far door.

'In there,' he muttered.

The armed man called to his colleagues, 'Through here!', and led the way.

They were followed by d'Avray, shouting impotently at them, 'A pox on you all, you bastards. May God's pox rot your bowels. What is it you want?'

Gates, still bringing up the rear, followed the rest into the third room. Though not himself quite a stranger to such places as this house, he was not so familiar with them that what he saw held no interest or amusement for him. Any bare-arsed man looked comic, even those who had not been caught in some extraordinary coil of coupling. The women's bodies, draped or not, were in some cases provocative to him, in others pathetic, or disgusting. In general, the effect upon Gates was to aggrandize the sense of confident power that he normally had. It put him in a good temper.

The third room was reserved for clients distinguished by class or by regular patronage. Those who had the privilege of using it were expected to leave a gratuity both for whore and house. It was divided into little cubicles, down each side of the long room. The privacy of the cubicles was created by screens or hanging draperies, which the armed men, now running along the central passage, were knocking and tearing down, to reveal the occupants.

Distraught at the ruin of his favoured premises and the damage to his custom, d'Avray followed, still shouting, 'I said, what do you want, you ruffians, damn your souls?'

It was in the very last cubicle that Guilford Dudley lay, in the lap of a whore twice his age. He was fast asleep. He woke up to find a sword held at his throat. Another was for his whore. Catching up, d'Avray saw the swords glinting in the candlelight, and fell silent.

'My Lord?' asked the armed man with the sword at Guilford's throat.

'Uh? Wha?' Guilford started to sit upright, but stopped when he felt the point of the sword. He looked at it both frightened and bewildered, and above all dead drunk.

'My Lord,' the armed man told him, 'you are to come with us.' He drew the sword back a few inches, to allow Guilford to sit up and find his clothes.

'Oh,' Guilford said. His eyes moved from the sword to its bearer. 'What?'

'Come with us.'

'What for?' Guilford was complying, without understanding. He pulled his hose up to his waist, and began trying to find the sleeves of his doublet.

Gates, beaming, stepped forward to the bed. 'My Lord,' he declared, 'congratulations. You are going to be married.'

Guilford looked up at him askance. 'Oh?'

Gates's face did not flinch. Everything save his eyes radiated joy at the announcement he had made.

Guilford nodded, twice, pursing his lips sagely. 'Oh,' he said, 'right', and he stood up to complete his dressing. As he laced up his doublet, a thought came to him. He paused and looked politely at Gates. 'To whom?' he asked.

In the main hall of Dorset Place food and drink had been set out on the long oak table. Six liveried attendants stood with their hands clasped in front of them. Frances and Henry Suffolk drank spiced wine while they waited. Mrs Ellen felt too nervous to take anything.

When Northumberland arrived he was served with a goblet of wine, while Mrs Ellen was sent to fetch the object of the happy occasion.

Jane was engrossed in the *Phaedo*, and not pleased to be told that she had to wait upon her parents in the main hall.

''Oh, my Lady,' Mrs Ellen assured her, 'I believe you shall think the time well spent.'

'Why?' Jane asked. 'What is it my parents want of me?'

'I may not say, my Lady.' Mrs Ellen's eyes were shining bright, and it was all she could do to contain the news. 'The Duke of Northumberland is with your parents, my Lady. Shall you wear the dress the Princess Mary sent you?'

'No, thank you, Mrs Ellen. If I must wear another dress than this one, please bring me my grey dress.'

'Very well, ma'am.'

In her dressing-room, Jane put on the severe, formal grey dress, with a plain collar of white silk. She tried again to draw Mrs Ellen on what was afoot, but her old nurse would not confide in her. Having no expectations of any pleasurable surprises from her parents, Jane was therefore still slightly tetchy when she descended the staircase and entered the hall. One look at her mother confirmed that an event of some importance was about to happen. On Frances's face was an expression that Jane had never seen there, something close to happy tears. Her father, too, was beaming with an unusual benignity, instead of the condescending, faintly bored look he usually wore when his eldest daughter greeted him.

'Good evening, Mother and Father,' Jane said.

'Jane,' Frances replied, hastening to take her daughter by the elbow, 'you know the Duke of Northumberland.'

'Of course I do,' Jane said. Only an effort of politeness prevented her from sounding impatient. 'My Lord.'

Northumberland came to take her hand, and incline his head.

'The Duke has some news for you,' Frances said, sounding weirdly girlish.

Whatever the news was, Jane by now was certain that it would be alarming. Since everyone was apparently waiting for her, she felt obliged to ask, 'What is it, pray?' A smile of anticipation was more than she could manage.

Her father cleared his throat. 'Jane, as you know, the Duke has fine sons.'

'Ye-es,' she replied. 'I have been privileged to meet with Robert, and, um –' She blamed herself for having forgotten the name, even if it was the name of someone she had not liked.

Frances reminded her. 'John.'

'Yes,' Jane said, with a little smile of apology, 'John Dudley, of course.'

'My third son', Northumberland told her, 'is called Guilford.'

'Guilford,' Jane repeated mechanically. She felt a trembling in her stomach. She knew now what all this must be leading to, and she prayed silently that she would have the courage to surmount it.

'It was his mother's maiden name,' Northumberland explained.

'Ah.' What were they doing to her? They had always wished her to marry Edward, and lately Edward had become dear to her, and she to him – of that she was certain. What few thoughts she had given to the matter of her marriage had all assumed that she would be Edward's wife, and everyone would be pleased by that. She was bewildered, miserable, and frightened. She swallowed. 'Guilford. I see.'

Frances, overcome by the tension, moved quickly to her daughter's side again. 'Oh,' she sighed, 'Jane.' With tears in her eyes, she put her arms around Jane and hugged her. 'Oh, my dearest little Jane.'

Jane could not remember the last time she had had her mother's cheek against hers. It was repellent. She felt herself captive in her mother's arms, and went rigid. 'Oh, Mother' was all she could think of to say.

Her father was attacking her now, arms outstretched, face wrinkled with smiles. 'My little girl,' he said, 'we are so proud of you, Jane, so proud.'

'No,' Jane said.

Frances understood her daughter to be so moved by the news that she could not believe her luck. 'Yes, yes,' she said, and grinned encouragingly.

'No.' Jane said it coldly, took a step back, away from all of them, and repeated it. 'No.'

Her parents exchanged a quick glance of concern. The girl's meaning was plain. Well, perhaps they should have expected some initial diffidence in her. She never had been spontaneous in her emotions, was always considered and cautious. They could explain that to Northumberland later. At present, Henry was anxious that the Duke be not offended. 'Now, Jane,' he bade her, 'embrace my Lord the –'

'No.'

The expressions congealed on every face save Mrs Ellen's. She was fighting down her tears.

After a pause, Frances asked. 'Jane, what is this?'

Henry was not going to argue it out with a girl of sixteen years of age. 'I order you –' he began.

Jane interrupted him by crossing the floor to the Duke of Northumberland, as her father had commanded. Instead of embracing him, she stood and addressed him. 'My Lord, I am most honoured – naturally. Certain it is that your son Guilford is the most noble of young men.' She clenched her fists, beside her skirt. 'But I do not wish to marry anyone at the present time. I do hope you understand.' Having said all that there was to say, she turned back to her parents.

Her father strode to her side and grabbed her arm, above the elbow, in a tight grip. 'You do not "wish"?' he shouted at her, then put his face close to hers. 'You do not "wish" to marry?'

'No, Father. I –'

'*I* wish it,' Henry shouted at her, still holding her arm painfully tight, 'and your mother wishes it, and the Duke wishes it, and King Edward –'

'No,' Jane gasped quickly. 'That I cannot believe.' She took advantage of the surprise her interruption had caused her father to pull her arm free.

'Oh,' Henry said sarcastically, 'oh, I see, you don't –'

'I do not believe the King wants me to marry Guilford Dudley.' She was relieved to hear that her voice had stayed firm, although all her body was trembling now, and she had to blink repeatedly if tears were not to start trickling down her cheeks.

Again a pause. Her father was nonplussed to be contradicted and so assuredly opposed by a bookish, unprepossessing girl. He would have liked to turn on his heel and leave the damned pack of them to sort it out amongst themselves. He had tried kindness, God knew, and persuasion, and all he had reaped was this stubborn, dumb, insolent child who thought she knew better than her elders. He was sick of the whole business.

Frances, on the other hand, was at her best when she did not have to feign a tender heart. She took control. 'Ellen,' she ordered, in a quiet, firm voice, 'take your mistress to the gallery.'

Jane spoke. 'No.'

Mrs Ellen looked distractedly from one woman to the other, and did not know what to do for the best.

Frances helped her to make up her mind. 'If you value your position in this household . . .'

Mrs Ellen turned to Jane, with apology on her face and grief in her heart. 'Um, my Lady?'

Jane took the initiative. She ran across the hall towards the doorway leading to the staircase. Mrs Ellen stumbled after her.

'Stop her,' Frances called coolly to the attendants. 'Take her.'

They did as they were ordered, moving to catch Jane by the arms. She struggled and kicked, but they were too strong for her, and held her head down low, until Mrs Ellen got to her.

'No, I will *not*,' Jane cried. 'I refuse to. I *will* not.'

Her cries grew fainter, to those in the hall, as the attendants and Mrs Ellen together managed Jane out of the door and through the long corridors of the house.

Frances, Henry, and Northumberland avoided each other's eyes. They had all been children, had all been coerced into doing what they would rather not have done, but none of them had ever behaved so disgracefully.

Frances was first to move, since she had work to do. She set her shoulders, and walked purposefully from the hall.

In the pause that gathered around her departure, Henry sought to make amends to Northumberland, who was expressionless. 'She will,' Henry assured him. 'Be sure of it, John. Her mother will see to it.'

Northumberland gave no indication of having heard Suffolk. He simply walked quickly away.

In a long, bare gallery of Dorset Place, for which no good purpose had been found since the friars once patronized by the family had been expelled from it, the attendants were holding Jane. She had now given vent to her tears, of anger and fear. Mrs Ellen stood beside her wringing her hands, unable to think of any words more consoling than 'There, there now'.

The door opened and Frances strode in. She was followed by an attendant carrying a long rod of birchwood. Striding up to her daughter Frances halted, feet astride, and asked, 'Well?'

Jane was beyond words. She closed her eyes, and shook her head.

'So be it,' Frances said, quietly. She nodded to the attendants. One fetched a stool. Jane was held over it, an attendant lifted the skirt of her dress and Frances, taking the rod, began to thrash her daughter. After four blows in succession she left a little time between each one, not to recover her strength, which was considerable even when it was not charged by spite, but so as to allow Jane the opportunity to sing out her repentance.

Northumberland, meanwhile, had hastened down to the river, where his pinnace had been waiting. He was swiftly rowed upstream to the landing-stage of Whitehall Palace, where he jumped ashore before the boat had made fast to the jetty. He went up the steps at a trot, past the bowing steward, and into the palace to find the King.

After being beaten for several minutes, Jane was left to think it over. She was held up in a slumped posture by the attendants. Her body was crumpled, her face tear-stained, and her will was shrieking within her like a mandrake root. Mrs Ellen stood at one side of the room, her presence there the only comfort she could offer.

Frances came back into the gallery, walked briskly over to Jane, and raised her face by pulling on her hair. 'Well?' Frances asked.

Jane's mouth opened, in a face wet with tears.

'*Well?*' Frances bellowed.

'I just,' Jane sobbed, 'I do not see why . . .'

Frances breathed in so sharply that it made a sound like a sigh in her throat. 'Then I must make you see why.'

Dropping Jane's head she nodded to the attendants, who brought Jane's body back over the stool. Frances held out her hand, was given the rod, and started to thrash her daughter again.

At the palace Northumberland had set himself a difficult task, but one which, after what he had witnessed, was imperative. The King had to be enlisted among those who would persuade the Lady Jane to marry Guilford Dudley. His influence was clearly decisive. The difficulty was that Northumberland could not, in all delicacy, explain to His Majesty precisely why the match was vital to the well-being of his realm.

At first Edward was reluctant to do as the Protector advised. 'You see,' he said more than once, 'my cousin trusts me.'

'And so she should,' Northumberland answered. 'That is the very reason why we look to you now.'

Edward frowned, not convinced, not easy in his mind about what he was asked to do.

'Your Grace,' Northumberland said, 'the battle is not won. I mean the battle started by your revered father, and now carried on by you. The reformation of your Church is incomplete. The awful danger that your country could fall back into the pit of Popery is still great. Every day brings fresh testimony to that risk.' When Edward turned to look him in the eyes, the Duke came close to saying what was really on his mind. Instead, rapidly, he continued, 'I cannot tell you why it matters that my son should marry the Lady Jane. But as she trusts you, and as you have trusted in all my counsels hitherto, all I can do is to beg your Grace to trust me now, in this.'

Edward's eyes stayed on Northumberland's face for a

moment. Then the King looked away with a wan smile. 'You had better send my attendants to me, to get me dressed.'

Northumberland sighed with relief, and smiled back at the wise young man. He bowed, and was turning to leave the room, when he heard the King say 'John'. He stopped, and turned around again, in surprise.

'I do know I am dying,' Edward said.

Jane was lying face down on the floor, by the stool. She had drawn her knees up towards her chest, and her arms were folded about her head. On the shift she wore under her dress, bright stains of blood were spreading. She was beyond sobbing, but her breast rose and fell with quick breath.

Frances had left her, and again returned, and again taken the rod from the attendant. Before using it she walked around her daughter's body and stood with her feet near Jane's protecting hands. She looked down. ' "I will not marry Guilford Dudley",' Frances said in a mocking voice. She stirred Jane's head with the toe of her boot, procuring at least the sight of her daughter's eyes. 'Who bought your books for you? Who paid your tutors, eh? Without your family, girl, what are you? Can you answer?'

Jane did not speak or move.

'I will give you your answer. No one. Nothing. Without your family, you are nothing. How can you dare to think that you may choose whom to obey?'

From the door Henry called. 'Frances!' His voice was urgent.

She looked up at her husband with baleful eyes, and almost shrieked, 'Yes? What is it?'

'Our daughter has a visitor.'

Frances glared at him. Before she could answer the King entered, formally dressed, with a sable-trimmed robe. He was followed by a servant carrying a basket.

Everyone bowed low. The King did not notice them. He was looking in dismay at the figure of Jane. She had opened her eyes to see who had come, and now was attempting to stand up to receive him.

'Your Grace –' Frances began.

Edward cut her off. 'We wish to speak, madam, with our cousin Jane. Alone.'

Frances and Henry, still bowing, left the room, followed by all the attendants. The King's servant left the basket on the floor.

'My Lady Jane,' Edward whispered.

'Your Grace . . .' she replied, in a little, hoarse voice. She tried again to get to her feet.

The King came quickly to her side. 'No, no,' he told her. He sat down beside her, on the dusty floor, and took her hand.

She let out a long, sobbing sigh. 'Oh, cousin, cousin.' She was surprised, and in some way pleased, to feel that she had tears left to come, hot on her cheeks.

'Now,' Edward comforted her, gently rubbing her hand in both of his, 'there, there.'

And she was comforted, and felt a first breath of calm over her body.

Edward talked to her. 'I wasn't whipped. They had a boy, and if I did something bad, they'd beat him instead of me. You should have been born heir to the throne.'

She looked up at him, smiling, and wept, her body shuddering with the relief.

'Though in a way it made it rather worse,' Edward

continued. 'You understand? But,' he shrugged, 'it was his duty, poor lad. As it was mine to suffer for that suffering of his, in my stead.' He squeezed her hand. 'As it is yours, now, to obey your parents' – he hesitated – 'and your King.'

The smile left Jane's face. 'Why must you do what that man tells you?' she asked.

'What man?'

'John Dudley.'

As kindly as he could, but wary of his dignity, the King replied, 'Because he has shown me that he has the interests of my country and of my faith at heart.' He paused for a moment, and added, 'Because I trust him.'

At Jane's crestfallen face, Edward changed tack. He walked over to the basket and fetched it back. 'Look. I brought you something.' From the basket he took out a marionette. He had had it dressed as a little nobleman, in doublet, breeches and cloak of velvet and fur.

'What is it?' Jane asked.

'It's a puppet. Look, you shake the cords, and it dances for you.'

She watched him make the man jig, and said, 'Let me.'

Taking the sticks in her hands, and raising herself on one hip, she too manipulated the little nobleman, and was delighted with the effect. 'Oh, look,' she grinned, 'it does. It works.'

'Of course it works,' Edward said, with a trace of the scornfulness he had had when they were small together, playing with childish things.

Accidentally Jane made the marionette bow to the King. They both giggled, and leaned forward closer to watch it on the floor. 'Look,' she said, 'it's easy.' And she produced another bow. 'He's bowing to you.'

'So I should hope.'

'Oh, Edward,' she said, 'it's –' She stopped herself at the inadvertence of using the King's first name. She glanced sideways at him. He hadn't minded. He glanced conspiratorially back at her. 'It's a wonderful present,' she continued. 'Thank you.'

The strings of the marionette had become tangled. He was stuck with one foot up in the air and his nose close to the ground. She let the sticks go, so that he fell flat.

Edward asked her, gently, 'All better now?'

'All better now,' she said.

His face was serious, as he took her hands in his again. He looked at her. 'Now promise', he said, 'that you'll marry him. Jane. For me. Will you?'

On her tear-stained face, shock was followed by pain, and her lips parted. She looked him in the eyes, and they both knew what she was thinking, what assumptions were finally being drained from her in this minute. Then she closed her mouth, half turned away her face, with a faint smile, and spread her hands. It was over now. She had lost.

# II

King Edward lay in a bedchamber at Greenwich Palace, in the state of half-sleep that drugs procure. His face was a pale creamy colour and bedewed with fever. When he coughed there was blood in his spittle, and an attendant with a napkin was always beside the bed to wipe it away. After leaving Dorset Place he had stumbled on the landing-stage, and might have fallen into the Thames but for Northumberland. Seeing how desperately tired the boy was, the Duke had unhesitatingly lifted him up in his arms, and borne him onto the royal barge. Frances and Henry had watched from the top of the steps, on their faces the satisfaction of having at last got Jane to see sense, after so much travail.

Northumberland was watching over the King. It was late in the evening, but Dr Owen had been sent for, in view of the King's deterioration. Northumberland repeatedly clenched and relaxed his fists, musing upon the King's racked face. There was still much to do, and every day, every hour, was precious time. It was ironic that people had been caught saying the King was ill because Northumberland had had him poisoned. No subject of the realm wished more ardently than Northumberland for His Majesty's continuance in this life. As long as the King could cling on, the crisis would be averted.

Time, and timing, were of the essence. The King had to write a last will excluding his sisters from the succession. He could not be expected to agree to that, not even be asked to contemplate it, while he might live for months. His respect for his late father's wishes, and his affection for his sisters, could not be put aside until he knew that he was approaching his end fast, and the needs of the realm, of which Northumberland would remind him, overswayed all else. As soon as he had signed that will, and it had been got through the Privy Council, the two bastard women could be seized, to prevent the popular uprisings in their favour which would otherwise surely follow. That business – the Council, then the seizures – would require a matter of some days: days during which any suspicion that the King was at the gates of death, or beyond them, would spark off the powder-keg prematurely, with incalculable consequences. That was why Lord Lieutenants and constables throughout the land had been instructed to pillory any loose mouth who was caught foretelling the coming death of King Edward. Prayers for His Majesty's early recovery from his present indisposition were offered up daily in every church.

Northumberland stood up and strode impatiently around the bedchamber, clenching, unclenching his fists. Where was Owen?

Rumour could not be enclosed. The preparations for Guilford's wedding to the Lady Jane had been seen by some cynics as a festive cloak to cover Northumberland's designs, or anyway to distract attention from the King's state of health. Not even the cynics were cynical enough to aver that Guilford Dudley's wife was to sit on the throne. No one gave any thought to the succession beyond the three children of King Henry VIII.

At last Owen was there. Northumberland said nothing until the physician had completed his examination. Then they left the chamber together, and in an anteroom Owen confided his opinion.

'Three days?' Northumberland's fists were clenched so tight they were shaking, with fury. He felt dreadfully betrayed, by mortality perhaps, but Dr Owen was more accessible. 'Three days?' the Duke growled in the physician's face.

Owen was not intimidated. He had been appointed to this position by Northumberland, who wanted confidentiality kept, and he saw no point in telling the Lord Protector anything but the truth. 'It could be four days,' Owen shrugged. 'Even a week, perhaps. No more.'

'We had him brought to Greenwich on your advice.'

'Yes,' the physician said. 'In the air of London he might have succumbed already.'

Northumberland was stroking his brow, muttering, 'It *must* be longer than that.'

'No.' Owen shook his head.

Pacing, beating his hands together, Northumberland repeated, 'It *must* be longer.'

He was addressing fate, but Owen misunderstood, and thought that the order was directed at him. 'The only thing is arsenic,' he said. 'It would stop the bleeding, and keep him more or less alive for a little longer possibly.'

Northumberland whipped around to face him. 'Well, then?'

'Arsenic, my Lord?'

'Yes. Do you not wish for the King's life to endure as long as possible?'

'I do, but not in those circumstances.'

'What circumstances?'

'If we administer arsenic, His Majesty will end his days in the most excruciating pain, my Lord.'

'Ah.' Northumberland nodded. 'There is nothing else?'

'No.'

'So be it, then.'

Again Owen misunderstood. He thought the Duke was resigning himself to divine Providence. But Northumberland was standing quite still, and looking expectantly at him, and slowly Owen realized what he had really meant. He was aghast. 'My Lord, you –'

'Doctor Owen. I must have the time. I *must* have it.'

To Dorset Place now came the dressmakers, the milliners, the jewellers, and the makers of spiced unguents that disguise the body's foul odours. Mrs Ellen had quite recovered her spirits. With a troop of handmaids recruited for the occasion she enthusiastically sorted through the lengths of wonderful stuffs the dressmaker had brought to show them. At each gasp of admiration Mrs Ellen would look up at Jane, hoping to see her approval given. Jane was there because it was required that she be there. She was not at all interested in what she would be dressed in at her wedding. Finally, because the business could not be done with until she had expressed some preference, she pointed to a plain indigo fabric. The dressmaker was holding it up against Jane when Frances entered, took one look, picked up a bolt of cloth-of-gold, and handed it to the dressmaker to settle the question. The jeweller's array of gleaming metals and glowing gems produced the same effect. While the other women were covetously trying on the rings and necklaces and bracelets, and holding the stones up to the light, Jane sat deep in a chair, eating a little spiced cake. Frances had to take responsibility for everything, and did not mind at all.

The wedding would be at Sion House, in Isleworth, the principal London residence of the Duke and Duchess of Northumberland. The Duke had it given out that King Edward would attend his cousin's wedding celebrations, and he took charge of all the arrangements. An altar cloth sewn with pearls was made for the chapel. Turkish carpets arrived at the house, and tapestries of Norman manufacture. The walls and the furniture alike were freshly upholstered in a tissue of gold and crimson.

At the instigation of his mother, whose favourite he had always been, Guilford agreed to meet his bride before the wedding day. When he was ready to leave Sion House, dressed soberly but richly, he suffered a momentary loss of nerve, and made for the sideboard. His elder brother Robert moved quickly to overtake him, and put his hand over the flagon of wine there, with a consoling but firm smile. Guilford stood still, biting his lip. Then he gave way with a good grace. The reason why was evident when he sat in a boat with his friend Thomas, being rowed downriver toward Dorset Place. Grinning, absurdly pleased with himself, Guilford put a hand inside his coat and brought out a flask of spirits. He removed the stopper, and raised the flask in salute to Thomas, who reached forward, took the flask from him and dropped it over the side of the boat. Guilford spent the rest of the journey slumped down in his seat, darting glances of reproach at his treacherous friend.

Their comradeship was perforce restored when Guilford, disembarking at the jetty of Dorset Place, set eyes upon his future parents-in-law. Frances, simpering a welcome, and Henry, doing something about a smile, stood at the head of a party come down to the river in greeting. Guilford stared, bowed, and turned half back to whisper to Thomas, 'God's teeth!'

Jane was watching from a high window, unseen by anyone.

The Suffolks led Guilford into their house, and invited him to sit down on a hard, high-backed chair. He was miserable. They had not even offered him a drink, a conceivable feature of the hour. Thomas went away with them, as interlocutor, and returned some ten minutes later. 'She wants to see you,' he told Guilford.

'Who does?'

'Your betrothed.'

Guilford swallowed, and felt scared. 'What, now?'

'Yes,' Thomas told him. 'Now.' He moved to one side, and behind him, framed in the doorway, was Mrs Ellen.

Guilford's jaw sagged. They had not warned him, not told him at all it would be like this – they had not played fair with him. He could not believe it. He beckoned hastily to Thomas and whispered frantically to him, 'Please, Thomas, tell me truly, this –' He cast a glance up to where Mrs Ellen was waiting for him. 'She can't be –'

Thomas controlled his mirth. 'No.'

Guilford was led through the house to a garden. He saw Jane at the far end of it, waiting on a seat. With Mrs Ellen and Thomas on either side of him, he advanced until he was twenty paces away. Then his escorts halted and withdrew to a seat of their own, by the brick wall, discreetly out of hearing but not of sight.

Jane knew what she wanted to say, and there was no reason to wait before saying it. 'I thought it right that we should speak together. You may have heard, my Lord, that I was most unhappy when I was advised of this match.'

'Yes,' Guilford answered. 'Yes, I did hear so.'

'I was made anxious by reflecting that my duties as a wife could interfere with what is important to me, that is to say, studying and prayer.'

'I see.'

'And so I would prefer, when this business of wedding is done, that we should live, let us say, as cousins, rather than as man and wife.'.

Guilford inclined his head. 'If that is your wish.'

'It is.' Having nothing more to say, Jane made a perfunctory curtsy and turned to leave him.

Guilford stayed her. 'But there is something that I myself should, perhaps, make clear to you.'

She paused and turned back. 'Please do.'

'On the night I was informed that I was to be translated into a husband, I had visited several taverns, beheld a bear-baiting, and was at that moment actually in the Southwark stews, sampling the pleasures afforded by a lady of the night. Thus far, I have to tell you, it had been a very good evening.' He pursed his lips, and looked up and down the prim figure, in severe black, of his betrothed. 'Still,' he shrugged, 'one has duties.'

With a vicious smile Guilford turned and left her. Thomas went with him.

Mrs Ellen walked eagerly across the garden to where

Jane was still standing. Her eyes were bright as she examined her mistress's face to gauge what effect the meeting had had upon her. When Jane said nothing, Mrs Ellen prompted her. 'Well, he's not bad looking, ma'am.'

'He is a person dreadful in every way,' Jane said. 'What matters it what his outward appearance be?'

Mrs Ellen's mouth was open. 'Well . . .'

But Jane was already walking haughtily back towards the house, observed from an upper window by her mother.

Archbishop Cranmer of Canterbury whispered a short prayer and raised his head. Below the pulpit the whole of the Dudley family and the Suffolk family were gorgeously attired, and behind them were the splendid ranks of the peers of the realm and the Privy Council. A gilded chair stood vacant to the left of Cranmer. King Edward would have been seated on it were he not indisposed.

'Dearly beloved,' Cranmer began, reciting the solemn words he had written himself, 'we are gathered together here in the sight of God, and in the face of this congregation, to join together this Man and this Woman in holy Matrimony; which is an honourable estate, instituted of God in the time of man's innocence . . .'

Guilford looked wonderful, in white velvets and silks, richly embroidered, trimmed with fur and glittering with gold adornments. He had been awoken that morning by Thomas, who drew back the curtains to admit warm spring sunshine, and greeted him, 'Good morning, my Lord. Now, can you guess what we have planned to do today?' Guilford grunted, stretched, yawned, sat up, then remembered, and had to have the bedclothes tugged off him.

'. . . and therefore is not by any to be enterprised, nor taken in hand, unadvisedly, lightly, or wantonly, to satisfy men's carnal lusts and appetites, like brute beasts that have no understanding; but reverently, discreetly, advisedly, soberly, and in the fear of God . . .'

Jane shone in the cloth-of-gold her mother had chosen. Diamonds, rubies and pearls had been sewn on to the full–sleeved robe, and her hair was braided with strings of pearls. Mrs Ellen had woken her, and while she was dressing Frances had come in to remind her of what they had told her the previous evening: the marriage was not to be consummated yet. Northumberland and Frances had agreed on that. It would be easier to undo the knots, should the course of political events alter and make the marriage unadvised. Jane had not asked the reason. It suited her well enough. She longed for it all to be over, so that she could resume her studies of Hebrew.

'Look mercifully upon these thy servants, that both this man may love his wife, according to thy Word, and also that this woman may be loving and amiable, faithful and obedient to her husband; and in all quietness, sobriety, and peace, be a follower of holy and godly matrons. O Lord, bless them both, and grant them to inherit thy everlasting kingdom . . .'

No one had woken the King Edward that morning, for he had not slept at all, but spent the night racked in desperate pain. His hands and feet were a whitish grey in colour. He prayed, out loud, for God to send him death.

It was Whit Sunday, and Cranmer read from St John's Gospel. 'And I will pray the Father, and He shall give you another Comforter, that He may abide with you for ever; even the Spirit of truth, whom the world cannot receive, because it seeth Him not, neither knoweth Him: but ye know Him; for He dwelleth with you, and shall be in you. I will not leave you comfortless . . .'

The service ended with prayers for the speedy recovery of His Majesty.

The wedding feast that evening was a select affair, staid, formal, and deadly dull. In the centre of it all sat Jane and Guilford, she in low spirits, he getting himself drunk as quickly and completely as he could. All around them sat the nobility of England, whose sombre expressions augmented the funereal gloom.

Between the tables a masque was being performed. Six coroneted virgins decked with flowers were blessing the union of Jane and Guilford, in a mixture of dance and mime which the Court dancing master was pleased to tell anyone who might listen that he had modelled on the antique Classic modes, as they were represented in the best Italian paintings. The song accompanying the masque might have sounded sweet, removed from the fustian setting. The rigmarole did little to cheer anyone up.

Guilford sustained his spirits by keeping an eye on Thomas, far down the line of tables, and exchanging winks and nods with him. When a serving maid came with a jug of wine, Jane put her hand forbiddingly over her dry goblet. Guilford quickly snatched it from under her hand, and held it out, together with his own, to be filled. He grinned happily at the maid, who bit her lip. Noble disapproval was registered on the faces around the incident. If Guilford noticed, he didn't care. He drained his own goblet, offered Jane's to her, shrugged when she turned her head away, and started to drink from it himself.

In a gallery overlooking the happy couple and their guests, Frances and Northumberland were sipping wine, and talking about the King's health.

'How long, then?' she asked.

'Two weeks,' Northumberland told her. 'Three at the most.'

Frances nodded thoughtfully. 'And has he yet declared his will, as it touches upon the succession?'

'I am confident that the King will act in the best interests of the new religion.'

'And what about his Councillors?' Frances looked without admiration at the Privy Council set out below her, bored, tired, saying scant words to their neighbours, mostly with minds bent on how soon they might decently take their leave.

Northumberland made a little smirk at Frances, and nodded down at the tables. 'They lack in understanding of some matters, but not of how much the rise of the new faith has contributed to their position. And their wealth.'

'Hm,' Frances said. 'Plain sailing, then.'

Northumberland looked thoughtfully down at the Earl of Arundel, now restored to his position on the Privy Council after serving a term of imprisonment in the Tower for his part in the Duke of Somerset's treacherous plots. That no such plots had ever existed had not deterred Northumberland from implicating Arundel in them. It was not to be expected that Arundel's present support for Northumberland would survive the first opportunity to betray him. 'No company numbering my Lord of Arundel ever sails plain,' the Duke answered Frances.

As the masque approached its grotesque climax Guilford, trying to gesture some ribaldry to Thomas, succeeded only in knocking over the crystal goblet before him in which some wine remained. He gazed fish-eyed at the dribbling wine, then called loudly for more to be brought. Jane, beside him, closed her eyes. When the serving-maid arrived Guilford took the full jug from her hands, filled both goblets, and set the jug on the table beyond the maid's reach. The maid, giggling but conscientious, tried to stretch out for the jug. Guilford intercepted her arm and waved her away. In doing so, he contrived to knock one of the full goblets over with such force that it hurled its contents into the lap of a duchess seated some way apart from Guilford, and smashed on the floor.

Henry Suffolk, who had joined his wife and Northumberland in the gallery, frowned. 'John,' he said, 'you are sure, aren't you, that you have chosen the right son of yours for my daughter?'

'I can control him,' Northumberland replied imperturbably. 'He can be controlled, when it shall come to matters that concern us, my Lord Duke.'

Amid the consternation that Guilford had caused, the duchess on her feet and flapping wine from her lap, surrounding noblemen exchanging raised eyebrows, servants rushing up with napkins, Guilford himself was not flustered. He took advantage of the attention he had attracted to wink broadly at one of the flower-bedecked maidens.

Jane noticed the wink. She took a spiced cake from

the table and bit sharply into it. To herself she swore a vow.

The virgins had a busy night. They were required to lead the bridal procession through the house to the bridegroom's chamber. First, in her own room, Jane was dressed in a nightgown and an elaborate arrangement of overgowns, scarves, and garlands. She stood quite still, and suffered it. Then the virgins set up a joyous warble, and lilted along the corridors. Jane followed. Behind her were Mrs Ellen, and Frances, and behind them a gossip of maids. The procession reached the anteroom leading to Guilford's bedroom, and there the virgins removed all Jane's deckings, leaving her white in a white gown. They sprinkled her with rosewater and perfumes.

Frances put her hands on her daughter's shoulders, and gave her a cold peck on the cheek. 'Remember,' she said warningly.

The virgins departed, with the maids. Frances followed. Mrs Ellen came forward to embrace Jane. 'Madam,' she said, 'you are sure that you understand . . .'

'Quite,' Jane said. 'There is no need, Mrs Ellen.'

Mrs Ellen left, and Jane stood alone, in front of the door to Guilford's room. She had never been alone with a man. Whatever happened, she had no intention or desire to consummate their marriage. But the man hidden behind that door was her husband until death. 'O God,' Cranmer had prayed, 'who . . . didst teach that it should never be lawful to put asunder those whom thou by Matrimony hadst made one', and Jane, seeing no other choice, had set herself the Christian task of finding and cherishing the human being within this animal. That was her vow.

She went into the room, closed the door quietly behind her, and stood, hands folded in front of her, looking demurely down. From the other side of the room came a groan, a snore, some noise. She looked up.

Guilford was splayed out on the bed, with his shirt on. One foot still wore a stocking and shoe, the other was entangled with a stocking, evidence of the point at which its wearer had abandoned the effort of undressing.

Jane crossed to the window. From the courtyard below she could hear the song the virgins had sung in the masque, but now rendered in a simple, pure voice. A serving-maid was carrying a tray of food towards the banqueting-hall. Probably it was for the virgins and the staff. The wedding guests had all gone home.

Behind her, she heard her husband's slurred voice. 'If I hear that damned tune again, I think I'll throw up. Again.'

Jane walked across to stand beside the bed, in an improvised formality of saying 'Here I am, your wife.'

He half opened his eyes, and regarded her. Then he responded by throwing his arms wide apart, in a pantomime of greeting. It was at once too much for him. He moaned, held his hands to his stomach, and rolled onto his side, away from her.

She looked down at the figure on the bed. She remarked how self-possessed she was feeling now, sufficiently so to feel a trace of pity for this wretched creature. She went to a washstand, moistened a cloth, and wiped Guilford's face with it. It seemed to soothe him. He slept quietly.

Hearing the song again, Jane went back to the window. The serving-maid, with an empty tray, was crossing back across the courtyard. Towards her a serving-man was carrying a tray full of jugs. He paused, looked around him, saw no one, put down his tray, and when the maid reached him he gently took her tray from her, placed it quietly on the cobbles, and took her in his arms. She kissed him back, passionately, running her fingers through his hair.

Guilford started to snore. At the window, a tear ran down Jane's cheek.

The Crown, in the person of Northumberland, had put Eversholt Priory, in the Chiltern Hills, at the disposal of the newly married noble couple, for as long as they had need of it, which meant until Northumberland should have need of them. It had fared better than most monastic institutions in the preceding years because it had not been sold off by King Henry to pay for the French wars. It still had lead on its roof. Its grounds had actually been enlarged by taking in some of the common land of Hertfordshire. The walls of the chapel, once vivid with biblical frescoes, had been whitewashed, and palimpsested with three lions rampant. The figure of the Blessed Virgin Mary had been destroyed and the jewels of her diadem now graced the head of a noble lady, whose breast glittered with the gems that had formerly adorned the roodscreen, and whose drawing-rooms were splendid with copes and altar clothes and chalices. The plain chapel, with its vacant niches and deal table, was perfectly suited to the needs of Jane's reformed temperament.

On the day they travelled there from London they saw the little village, dominated by the Priory, from the top of a hill, and Jane asked the coachman to halt. They stepped down from the coach, Jane to enjoy the view,

Guilford to lean, bored, against the coach.

'It's beautiful,' she said.

'Yes, m'Lady,' the coachman said.

Guilford stretched his shoulders, and said nothing.

Jane turned to her husband and, as though it were a challenge, asked him, 'Don't *you* find it beautiful?'

Guilford glanced into the valley, sniffed, stretched his shoulders again, and said nothing.

She regarded him with fury. She would not be dismissed so easily. For the present she had no more experience to draw upon, in this circumstance, than the game she had played with Elizabeth, as a child. She did not hesitate to use it. With a little sigh, her hand to her forehead, she crumpled to the ground.

Still leaning against the coach, his arms folded, Guilford half turned his head to look at her, and sniffed again.

She remained quite still on the ground. The coachman turned, with an anxious look, and started to get down from his seat.

Then Guilford sprang forward, ran to Jane, and knelt down beside her. 'What's the matter with you?' he said.

Her breath was short, and her body twitched.

Guilford looked up wildly at the coachman. 'What am I supposed to do?' he asked. He attended more urgently to his wife. 'Jane. What is the matter? Jane?'

As suddenly as she had crumpled, she sat up, brushing the sleeves of her gown, and smiled brightly at him. 'Better now,' she said.

He regarded her for a moment, to be sure. Her smile was unequivocal. He was furious now. His callow adolescence could not cope with her trick. Like her, he reverted instinctively to the behaviour he had learned all his life, until the preceding few months. He leaped upon her, to wrestle for his revenge.

They rolled over together on the turf, each with anger to expend. Against his strength her determination was matched. And besides, something else saved her from being forced to submit. Locked in each other's arms, for the first time, they could hardly fail to feel a sensation which distracted each of them from anger and punishment.

Guilford it was who broke away and stood up quickly. He brushed himself down, and did not look at her. She did likewise. Engrossed in removing little blades of grass from their clothes, they climbed back into the coach.

Further on along the road winding down the hillside toward Eversholt, the coach came abruptly to a halt. Jane and Guilford looked out. They saw a group of peasant men around the coach, dressed in drab and tattered garments. One of them had brought the coach to a halt by seizing the bridle.

'What is this?' Jane asked. She had never seen such people, their faces so surly. She was sure they were up to no good.

Guilford shook his head. 'I've no idea.' He stepped down from the coach and to the peasants said, 'Good day. Is there anything you want of us?'

The men did not answer. They were looking at the coach as though it offended them, and one or two kicked spitefully at the wheels. The coachman did not think it proper for him to reproach them, but waited for Guilford Dudley to do so. From behind a hedgerow came a couple of women, in no better attire than their menfolk, and with no more agreeable expressions on their faces. With them were a few ragged children, nothing on their feet.

Inside the coach, Jane was now thoroughly frightened. She had heard tell of coaches held up by robbers, but all her travelling had been done with parents and servants in attendance, and nothing like this had ever befallen them. It was such a lovely spring day. Why could these people not enjoy God's gifts, instead of roaming about making trouble and spoiling people's lives?

Guilford was still trying to engage the men in conversation. 'My wife and I have come to stay here. At the Priory. It is a great pleasure for us.'

Still he got no answer. The men were whispering among themselves, never looking him straight in the eye.

He took a purse from his doublet. 'And as a token –' he started to say.

Before he could finish, the purse was snatched from his hand. The man who had it held one hand cupped and poured the coins out from the purse. The others gathered round to inspect the money.

Suddenly the man with the coins used his free hand to rip open the worn piece of drab cloth that served him as shirt. On his chest was a large, livid scar in the shape of a B. 'You know what that is?' he asked.

Now all the other peasants were looking at Guilford's face. With a dry throat, he replied, 'Yes. You've been branded.'

Jane's face at the window of the coach was white.

'Why?' the man asked, tilting his head so that his jaw was thrust out.

'For begging, I suppose,' Guilford answered.

'That's right.' The man had not expected a fine creature like Guilford to know the answer. Branding was a job done by stewards and the like, while Guilford's sort were within their great house, drinking wine from golden chalices. But the man's ire was not deflected. He drew back his hand and flung the coins into Guilford's face. 'We don't want alms. Give us our land back.'

Guilford stepped forward and seized the man by the arm, hoping to restrain and reassure him at the same time. 'It is not our fault,' Guilford said. 'Leave us – my wife and me – alone.'

'Not your fault? Whose is the fault, then?'

'Not ours.'

'If you do not own the fault, you do not own the land.'

'We are visitors. We have not come to stay for long. There is nothing we can do for you.'

'Huh.' The man was sceptical, but his temper appeared to have gone off the boil.

Guilford let go of his arm, and turned back toward the coach. The children had been scrabbling on the ground for the coins. When Guilford turned towards them, they darted away. One of them dropped a coin, eyed it for a moment, then ran off. Guilford picked it up. He was about to toss it to the nearest child when he changed his mind and put it in the pouch on his belt. He climbed back into the coach. Jane looked at him, her face drained. He looked blankly at her. There was nothing to say.

The coachman shook the reins, and as the coach moved forwards the peasants parted to make way. Their faces, looking in at the windows, were dark with despair.

Outside the gate of the Priory a servant in plain jacket and breeches was waiting to open the door of the coach and hand Jane down. She ran straight into the courtyard, as though into a haven. At doorways and windows a few rustically dressed maids and serving-men were standing, with solemn faces, but in the middle of the courtyard Mrs Ellen, who had been there for some days, was smiling and holding her arms open in welcome. Jane hugged her. 'Oh, Mrs Ellen, this is lovely. Is there anything to eat?'

'Yes, of course there is,' Mrs Ellen chuckled. Over Jane's shoulder she watched Guilford slouch into the courtyard, looking about him as though he had no great hope of anything he might be pleased to see. No one went to greet him.

As Mrs Ellen took Jane into the house, Guilford stood in the middle of the courtyard, seeing the dour country faces that were seeing him. Then he sauntered on towards the doorway through which Mrs Ellen had taken Jane. He found them in a parlour. A plate of spiced cakes was on the table, and Jane was eating hungrily. He stayed by the door, leaning. He shook his head when Mrs Ellen brought the plate of cakes to him. 'Um,' he said, 'tell me, where is the nearest town?'

'Oh,' Mrs Ellen replied, 'twenty miles hence, I should expect.'

'I see. How long are we supposed to stay here?'

'Oh, a month, I think, my Lord, as I was told. A month at least.'

'Very well,' Guilford said, and 'Yes', and he closed his eyes, as though in a moment of pain. He opened them again and watched Jane. 'Does she always eat like this?'

Mrs Ellen looked at Jane with a fond smile. 'Since childhood.'

'Since?' Guilford looked as if he were about to

collapse under the weight of tedium, slide slowly down the wall and settle in a tired heap. Instead he straightened, took a breath, set his shoulders bravely, and stepped away from the door. He addressed Mrs Ellen. 'I have to tell you I am in constant hope of awakening to find that all this has been no more than a nightmare. I am praying, mistress, that you and she are merely figments of a brain which, I confess it, I have sorely heated of late. I have beheld stranger visions, in my cups. Perchance this will prove to be another such, though less entertaining.'

With a curt bow he spun on his heel and went out to the courtyard again, seeking he knew not what.

The rest of that afternoon yielded nothing to Guilford more diverting than watching his wife eat cakes. He wandered around the grounds of the Priory, at which Jane had exclaimed ecstatically from the hilltop, and the most amusing companions he could find were three sheep. When he sat down in front of them they stopped chewing for a while, and watched him carefully. Their faces were as glum as his. He tried to cheer all four of them up by contorting his face, tongue stuck out sideways, eyes askew, but the sheep missed the point. They went on waiting to see if he would do something else, and when he didn't they bent their three heads back to the grass. Guilford frowned, sighed deeply, and stood up again, looking all around for something to do that was better than nothing. On a terrace of the Priory building Jane was reading a book. Beside her were Mrs Ellen and two maids, all sewing. Guilford watched for a while, then turned back to the three sheep. This time they did not so much as glance up at him. He looked around the horizon, and eventually his gaze returned to the women on the terrace. A little breeze had blown a lock of hair across Jane's brow, and she brushed it away, without taking her eyes from the book. To Guilford the slight gesture was endearing. He could not understand why. He continued to watch his wife, from a distance. She was not aware of him, absorbed as she was in the Hebrew of Ezekiel, about which she intended to correspond with her intellectual admirers in Zürich.

They dined in the parlour that evening. Jane ate heartily, Guilford drank as much as he decently could, given that there were but the two of them at table, and half a dozen servants waiting upon them. Already he felt that this was Jane's house, the people Jane's people, and he was on his mettle. Their conversation, desultory and distant, was about the Priory. They did not seem to have any other interest in common.

'Well,' Jane said, 'in my opinion it is quite delightful. The King is most generous to allow us the use of it.'

'Oh, yes,' replied Guilford, one arm over the back of his chair. This little pious person, his wife, invited a sardonic answer to everything she said. Fiddling with his glass goblet, he said, 'I doubt if the poor old monks appreciate the King's generosity, having been pitched out of their home.'

Jane spoke levelly. 'The "poor old monks" were trumpets of the Antichrist.'

'Oh, yes,' Guilford said, 'of course they were.'

Since there was nothing more to say about that, Jane signalled to a servant to carve the leg of lamb.

Guilford watched her. He imagined how it would be to hear the clatter of hooves outside, Thomas and Richard charging in to rescue him, the wild laughter as they galloped through the night, back to London. He could send a letter commanding them to do it. No, he couldn't. His father would have them all thrashed. For himself, it might be worth a thrashing, but his friends would not dare to cross his father's purposes. He was marooned in this place. He thought he would go to sea, when he could. The present time was to be endured. He made a small effort. 'So,' he remarked, 'we are on our own.'

Jane swallowed her mouthful. 'We won't be tomorrow.'

'What?' Guilford's eyes shone.

She nodded. 'The Mayor of Hertford is to dine with us in the refectory.'

'Ah.' Hopefully, Guilford enquired, 'Just the Mayor?'

'His Worship will be accompanied, I believe, by several of the aldermen of Hertford.'

Guilford's eyes unfocused again. 'God's teeth,' he muttered.

Jane looked at him reproachfully, with a little pout.

He had to do something back to her, this complacent, self-contained, sanctimonious, omnivorous little body. Mischievously he held up in finger and thumb his empty glass goblet, one of an elegantly stemmed set, brought from Venice, that his family had given them. 'Very fine glass,' he observed, holding the goblet even more delicately.

'Yes. They are pretty.'

'They are pretty,' Guilford agreed, 'but such fine, pretty things do have one disadvantage, don't you think? They are very easily broken.'

Jane stopped chewing and stared at the goblet,

precariously poised in his fingers. 'Don't you *dare*.'

She glared, he smirked. He put the goblet down on the table again with exaggerated care. She took no notice. That was that. He had got all the entertainment he was going to get from his threat. Another minute of time had been passed. God's teeth, he thought, slumped in his chair. He took out a coin, and fiddled with it.

Jane was helped to pease pudding. 'Those men, on the hillside beyond the gates,' she asked. 'What was it that they wanted, do you suppose, since it was not apparently to take our money?'

'I don't know. Food.'

'Have they no farms?'

'I'm sorry?' Guilford said, not understanding her question.

'Have they no farms?' she repeated.

He looked straight at her, dumbfounded. How was it possible to live in the world, even in the noble world, even in the world where one corresponded with learned Calvinists in Switzerland about the fine points of Hebrew syntax, and know so little? In the taverns and the cockpits and the stews, in society and at home with his family, Guilford had never thought that anything except pleasure was worth taking seriously, but even he had not failed, wherever he went, to hear snatches of conversation and argument about the kingdom's plight. Was a girl so cosseted in her upbringing that nothing at all of it ever reached her ears? He set about informing her with a certain savage relish, compounded of an escape from boredom, slight tipsiness and, he recognized it, a desire to hit back and wound this invulnerable righteousness of hers. 'What do you mean?' he asked.

She looked at him as though he must be stupid. 'Why

are they idle?' she asked in her reasonable voice. 'Have they no work to do?'

'Did you see his chest?' Guilford asked.

'Yes. It was marked.'

'No, it wasn't. It was branded. That "mark" you saw had been burned into him, with a red-hot iron. And do you know why?'

She shook her head.

'Because he had been caught begging. Begging. And can you think how he might have fallen into beggary?'

Jane's lips tightened as she recognized that he was attacking her for her ignorance. 'No.'

Her tightened lips aroused Guilford. He had pierced her defences. With a passion that was transubstantiated into anger about the conditions he was describing to her, he went on, 'Because the land he used to farm, on which he used to have much work to do, actually belonged to poor old monks in poor old monasteries who allowed poor people like himself to plant their crops and grow their food. As well as other things the monks did, such as healing their sicknesses, and teaching their sons – trumpets of Antichrist, sounding brass though they were, my Lady. All that they did for the poor, until my father, and your father, and men like them, stripped the monasteries, smashed the windows, carried off the paintings and the tapestries to decorate their own great houses, enclosed the common land with fences, drove the peasants from their own fields, and then passed those unholy laws which brand the poor for beggary.'

'But –' Jane said, trying to gather her thoughts, which were as much confused by finding that Guilford had feelings and knowledge and the power to express them as by the injustice he described.

'Laws which burn a man's flesh for wanting to eat when he is hungry, but of which it seems you are quite ignorant.' He paused. 'That is why they stopped us. They might have done worse. They have elsewhere. But not in the Manor of Bradgate, evidently.'

'But you –' Jane began, looking for the words, 'you gave them all that money, and they just, they threw it back . . .'

'Money?' Guilford was leaning forward in his chair, his hands flat on the table. 'Do you not know what is happening to the value of the coinage?'

'No,' Jane said in a small voice. She was frightened.

He found the coin he had been fiddling with, the same one he had put back in his pouch that afternoon. He thrust it at her. 'What's that?' he demanded.

She took it from his hand and looked at it. It was small, ill-shaped, and tarnished. 'A penny.'

He shook his head emphatically. 'No it's not. It is a shilling piece.'

She looked at him, puzzled. 'It cannot be. Shillings are made of silver.'

'They should be made of silver,' he told her. 'They used to be. Not any more. That is why a shilling is not worth a shilling now.' He took the coin back from her, relaxed into his chair, and regarded her with a twist of his lips, the weary cynic watching the embattled innocent. Slowly, he said, 'You have no conception about what is happening in the world, have you?'

It was true, and she knew it, but not for anything would she surrender without a fight. And so, sitting up straight with dignity, she chose the ground on which she was confident of winning. 'I know the priests were all corrupt.'

'No doubt.' Guilford's shrug said, So what?

'They told the credulous people that they must worship icons, and mumble spells.'

'Now that concerns me less.'

Slowly, Jane told him, 'It ought to concern you very much. What you are talking of is your soul.'

'No,' Guilford replied, 'you are talking of your mind. And I do wonder sometimes if you – and all the grand reformers – couldn't talk yourselves into believing that the question of the number and the nature of the sacraments was really more important than whether the people who receive them live or die.' He picked up the goblet again, this time in two hands, with his thumbs placed on the slender stem as though he were going to break it. 'The brain's a brittle organ, Jane. The slightest pressure, and it snaps.'

She was watching his hands.

'What saves it is to wrap it up in a little heart.' He held the goblet in one hand, upright, and signed to a servant to bring the jug of wine.

Jane was furious to have her beliefs mocked. By *him*. She doubted if he knew a word of Greek or Hebrew: more darkly doubted if he truly knew Jesus Christ; yet, instead of entering into argument with her, he had the gall to sit there, drinking to get drunk again no doubt, and airily dismiss her with his knowing shrugs and smiles, and then think himself the man to offer her this little homily upon a wineglass. She stood up. 'I think – I shall have them arrange another bedroom, for me.'

Guilford pursed his lips. 'They won't approve of that.'

'I couldn't care less what they approve of.' She walked briskly towards the door, which a servant opened for her. Before going out she paused and turned back.

Passionately, her fingers squeezed in the palms of her hands, she asked, 'What right have *you* . . .? You haven't done a thing. Why don't you go to Court, become a Secretary, or a Councillor: do something about all these injustices you've remarked?'

'Because . . .' Guilford reflected for a moment, knowing that she would wait for his reply. 'Because there isn't any point. Because it would not have any effect. Because it never has.'

Across the room they glared challengingly at each other. The ground of their dispute had little to do with politics or religion. What was in question was how much territory each would concede to the spirit of the other. Until this evening neither had expected that there would be any encroachment at all. A marriage had been arranged. Both were a little frightened now.

When Guilford leaned back in his chair and cried out, to the ceiling, 'Dear God and all His saints, what am I doing here?', it was not the cry of a bored despair that it would have been that afternoon, but a sincere interrogation, if not of the Almighty then of himself.

Jane continued to glare at him for a moment, certain that there was something more to say. When it did not come to her, she turned and marched away. The servant closed the door behind her.

Guilford had not watched her leave. As nonchalantly as he could he reached for the jug and filled his goblet. The surface of the wine was trembling a little as he lifted it to his mouth.

Jane went through with her determination to have a separate bedroom. Guilford saw where the maids were taking the fresh linen sheets, and then he went out to clear his head and calm himself, pacing up and down in the chilly springtime night, under clear stars, and glancing indecisively up at the glowing window. When he judged that it was time, he went back into the house and upstairs, into the small anteroom leading to Jane's bedchamber. He strode up to her door, raised his fist to knock upon it, then changed his mind, turned, and walked away.

He changed his mind again, turned back, and knocked before thought could deflect him.

She was sitting up in bed, propped by pillows, reading. Beside her was a bell that would summon a chambermaid, or Mrs Ellen.

Guilford shut the door behind him. The draught caused the bedside lamp to flicker, and giant shadows danced on the walls. He remained at the door, leaning against it, ready to leave again on the instant.

'What do you want?' Jane asked.

'I want to say that I am sorry.'

'It doesn't matter.' She looked down at her book.

'Yes it does matter. This . . .' – he made a small gesture, meaning the predicament in which they found themselves – 'this is no fault of yours.'

'That's true,' she said primly. After a brief pause, 'Well, then. Good night.'

Guilford closed his eyes, and stayed where he was. She bent her head over her book. The lamplight was shining through her dark hair.

'Explain it to me,' Guilford asked, quietly.

'My book?'

'No.'

'What, then?'

'What it is you believe: the schism, the new learning,

the nature of the sacraments.' He took a couple of steps towards her, and on his face she could just make out a wry smile of apology. 'I slept through all the sermons. I did not think they would ever touch upon my life.'

'And do you now think that they do?'

'Now that your life touches upon mine, yes.'

'And you really want to know?'

With a meekness that took him by surprise as much as his anger earlier that evening had, Guilford answered, 'Yes. I really want to know.'

She closed her book and laid it aside. He took that to be an invitation to approach her bed and sit upon it.

'Well,' she began, smiling solemnly at him, 'it is our belief that faith alone saves. That as Christ Jesus says, His sons shall come to God if they believe in Him.'

'Come to Him not by the Church?'

She nodded. 'Not by the Church. We say that men may speak to God through prayer, and without their needing the intercession of priests.'

'Yes. Yes.' Guilford leaned forward.

'And that all superstitions, ornamental relics, icons, images, false . . .' Her voice ceased as her mouth closed on his. She leaned forward to put her arms around him, and her long hair, brushed out by Mrs Ellen, fell over her cheeks. Her hand behind his neck was stroking his hair.

Guilford was leaning forward on his hands, and stayed so for a time. When he put one arm around her shoulders, the weight of his body leaned them both down to the pillows. Jane's hand stopped stroking his hair. She did not move at all, although her mouth was on his, until he raised his head a little to murmur, 'Go on.'

'Go on?' she asked, in a small, dry voice.

'With what you were doing.'

'With what I was saying?'

He could feel her deep, long breathing below him. 'Not . . . just now,' he told her.

She gently stroked his cheek, and held him slightly away to see him better. At the corner of her eye, a tear ran down. Smiling, she shook her head. 'What do I do?' she asked.

In the morning light Guilford asked her, 'When did you know?'

'I didn't know. It just happened. I thought I didn't even like you at all.'

'There's no shame in that.' He sat up and stretched his arms.

'In not having liked you?'

'In finding that you did.'

She turned her face to one side. 'I suppose not.'

'I was in the same way,' he said.

'Yes. I knew that.'

'It seemed to be your determination that I should not like you.'

'Yes. It was.'

'Why?'

'I don't know. It was too strange. And then . . .'

'What?'

'It would have pleased my parents, it seemed to me.'

Guilford nodded. He could understand that. 'And,' he went on, 'did you know about what we've just done together?'

'Well,' Jane said, 'only in terms of the broadest, most general principles. Unlike you.'

'Ah. Well, not exactly.'

She looked at him curiously.

'You are referring to my lady of the night.'

'Yes.'

'Passed out.'

'What?'

'I did. Passed out. I got to the bed, then – nothing. I forget. A complete failure. A terrible embarrassment. At least, I suppose it was, except that I quite forget it all. Why are you crying?' Guilford asked.

'Don't you know?'

'No, of course I don't.'

'I was the first,' Jane said.

'Ah.' Guilford smiled. 'You are the first.' He stroked her cheek with the back of his fingers.

She did not look at him. 'And will I be the last?'

He put his face close to hers, and kissed her tears. 'Why should I seek another?'

Tongues were clacking all over London that the King was mortally ill. Until he had settled his succession such rumours were as sparks to gunpowder, and so bulletins were issued daily that His Majesty had enjoyed a pleasant walk in the grounds of Greenwich Palace, and his convalescence was proceeding most effectively in the clear country air. When Sir Hugh Willoughby's squadron, under the ordinances of Sebastian Cabot, sailed from Greenwich in search of a north-east passage to Cathay, the King was there to wish them God-speed. Northumberland had two footmen hold the King up at a window, a shaking, ghastly puppet, his waving hand worked by one of the footmen. Twelve months later Willoughby and his entire ship's crew would be found, frozen to death, by a fisherman off the northern coast of Russia.

Edward was carried back to bed, and laid against the

pillows. As his hands were too withered to be of any use to him, Dr Owen held the potion of arsenic to his lips to drink, then wiped the King's mouth and chin with a napkin.

Edward waited until the physician and footmen had left the chamber before resuming his discussion with Northumberland. To the boy's physical distress was added the emotional pain of what the Duke insistently proposed to him. 'My revered father's will is quite clear,' Edward said, not for the first time. He groaned, loudly, with the effort of drawing breath. His suffering, and Northumberland's adamantine will, had reduced him to the point where he could do no more than mouth his objections from memory.

Northumberland sensed that he was close to his goal now, and he gathered together all the arguments that he had been putting for weeks. 'It is no less clear, your Grace, that the Princess Mary would deliver your realm back into Popery. The cause for which you have worked all your life will be wasted.'

'She is my sister,' Edward said.

Northumberland leaned forward and spoke, quietly and deeply, close to the King's ear. 'But, your Grace, it is the sacred duty of a Christian king to set aside the prejudices of the blood in favour of the greater good, which is his God and his country. Or else – for our life on earth is short, your Grace – he will answer for it at the dreadful seat of judgement.'

Edward's eyes, which had been looking at the Lord Protector with a sort of haggard trust, closed. 'Elizabeth?' he asked, in a voice that was rather asking to be reminded and reassured than putting a question.

'The Princess Elizabeth's rights are not divisible from

the Princess Mary's, your Grace. If the elder sister may not succeed, in logic the younger may not, either. Moreover, it is certain that either of your sisters would find no husband worthy of her in the realm, and that she would be married to a foreign prince. It would end with the extinction of the very name of England, an outcome with which I cannot think your Grace would be content.'

'Then the next in line of succession would be the Lady Frances of Suffolk.'

'Yes – who, as your Grace has already been advised, has ceded her right of succession, leaving her daughter, the Lady Jane, to enjoy the right. I do not need to remind your Grace what affectionate sympathy there has always been between yourself and the Lady Jane. I cannot believe there is a soul in England to be better trusted than hers to persevere in the work of reformation to which you, after your revered father, have devoted so much labour and prayer. She is married to my son, of course, but I am content that they be bound by oath to perform whatever your Grace shall decree. I do not consider my own interest in the business, but the benefit of the whole kingdom.'

Dr Owen, concerned for his patient, came back into the chamber to examine him. Edward's face turned on the pillow to look at him. The deep breath he sucked in rasped in his throat, and was exhaled with a long whimper. Dr Owen looked from the King's face to Northumberland's, and could not bear what he saw. He turned and left again, shaking his head in distress.

'Consider, your Grace,' the Duke said, 'what answer you shall give at the dreadful seat of judgement, when you are called to account for the consequences of your actions on this earth.'

Edward looked at him, piteously. 'The devise of succession, my Lord – have you a draft of it?'

The document was in Northumberland's hand. He laid it on the King's lap.

Edward murmured aloud the first words of it. 'To the Lady Jane and her heirs male. The throne of England, Ireland, France.' He closed his eyes, and held out his hand to Northumberland for a quill.

Quill and inkpot were in readiness beside the bed. The Duke dipped the point and carefully placed the quill in the withered and horribly discoloured hand.

'Yes,' Edward muttered, and moved the quill across the foot of his will in the best simulacrum he could manage of his signature. It was really no more than a child's scribble in imitation of what it sees its elders do with a quill, but it would serve the purpose. Having done it, he lay back on his pillows.

Northumberland took the quill and the document from the King's lap, and stood up.

'Oh, John,' Edward groaned.

'Your Grace?'

'I want this to be over.'

Northumberland nodded, and gently patted the King's shoulder. He held the document tightly in his hand as he left the chamber.

Outside, Gates was waiting for him, with Dr Owen, other physicians, and a clergyman. Gates looked questioningly at the Duke's face, set in stern lines.

'I want the Privy Council called,' Northumberland told him.

'Yes, my Lord.'

'And I want forces ready to take the Princesses Mary and Elizabeth, the moment this is countersigned by the Council. I want them standing by, you understand?'

Gates nodded, and left at once.

Northumberland was about to follow him when his arm was seized by Dr Owen. 'Please,' the physician begged, 'now, please may we –'

'Yes,' Northumberland answered. 'Let him die now. Yes.'

At Eversholt Priory the refectory table had been set for eight. Guilford entered, formally dressed in silk and velvet, with golden decorations, and was surprised to find himself quite alone. Not even the servants were there yet, even though food was ready on the table. He sat down, poured himself a goblet of wine, and sipped it while he waited. He thought he ought to be offended. The Mayor and aldermen should certainly have been waiting upon him, and the absence of all servants must be some aberration of the chief steward. It would have been normal, also, for Jane, with Mrs Ellen, to have preceded him. He took another sip of wine, and grinned to himself. He was in far too high a good humour to be offended.

Nevertheless, when Jane appeared he went through a mime of frowning at her, as he stood up. His frown became one of perplexity when he saw, as she came into the circle of candlelight, that she was dressed in a simple blue gown, without any jewellery save her wedding ring.

'What is going on?' he asked. 'Where are they? His Worship the Mayor and all his worthy aldermen.'

'Oh,' Jane answered lightly, 'I sent word that we were

unwell, and could not receive them.'

Guilford giggled, and sat down again. 'They won't approve of that.'

Gaily she replied, 'I couldn't care less what they approve of.'

She sat down, and both of them were infected with laughter. Subsiding, he looked across the table at her, and said, 'Who is this woman?'

'What?'

He rested his chin on his hand. 'I don't know who you are.'

'No more do I,' Jane said.

He went on gazing at her for a while. Then his face became quizzical. He filled his goblet, one of the Venetian ones with a red pattern in the slender stem, and asked her, 'All right, tell me what you want.'

'What do you mean?'

'If you could have any wish,' he said, 'what would it be?'

'Love, to be with you.'

'No. Not a wish for us. I mean, what would you wish for the rest of the world?'

'Well . . .' Her face was thoughtful. 'I would wish, if I could have anything . . . our country to remain true to the faith of God, as it has been revealed to us in Scriptures.'

'Good,' Guilford said at once. He picked up his goblet full of wine, held it out over the stone floor, and dropped it. As it smashed, he said, 'Then it's done.'

Her eyes were popping out. What Guilford had just done was the most simply shocking thing she had ever seen done.

He reached out for another goblet, filled it with wine,

and pushed it across the table to his wife. 'Now it's my turn,' he said. 'Ask me.'

'Ask you what?' she said, in a nervous tone.

'Ask me what I want,' he told her happily.

'What do you want?'

Guilford sat back, his hands clasped behind his head, and thought. 'I believe, you know, that it is this . . .' He paused again, because the game was a serious one to him, and he wanted to be sure that his angry passion of the previous day had not been merely a posturing but had left a residue of conviction. 'I think that what I want is a world where men are not branded or sent into slavery because they can't grow the food they need to eat.'

Jane was looking at him.

'Go on,' he urged her.

She shrugged. 'Oh well . . .' She took the goblet from the table, held it away from her, and let it smash on the floor. She stared at the shards of glass, the creeping rivulets of wine. 'It's done,' she said.

Guilford was pouring wine into a third goblet. 'So what else, then?' he asked. 'Death to all bishops, cardinals, and popes, should it be?'

Jane said, 'An end to their power over men's and women's souls.'

He dropped the glass. 'It's done.'

She pushed her empty goblet across the table to him. He filled it and returned it. 'And an end,' he wished, 'to the power of kings and princes, and dukes, over men's bodies and their minds.'

'It's done.' The fourth goblet dropped from Jane's hand.

Guilford stood up and walked around the table, filling the four goblets that remained. 'And for a world where the happiness and comfort of a few are not bought by the misery of many,' he said.

She responded, 'And where children are not beaten and cajoled but loved and nurtured.'

'And where men shall live in peace upon God's earth, as it is written in the Scriptures.' He watched her, waiting for her to express her last wish.

'And,' she said, after a pause, 'where every man and woman might feel a half, a quarter, oh – the merest iota, of what I feel for you.'

He picked up one of the glasses, and let it drop. 'It's done,' he said, his voice matter-of-fact.

Jane stood, and went to smash a sixth goblet. 'It's done.'

He held the next goblet above the table. When it smashed there, glass and blood-red wine glinted in the candlelight. 'It's done.'

She did likewise. 'It's done.'

'It's all done,' Guilford said. 'Now tell me, my love, was that so hard?'

The door was opening and Mrs Ellen came in, worrying. 'What on earth is going on?'

They both turned to face her. 'Ah,' Jane said, 'Mrs Ellen.'

'Mrs Ellen,' Guilford said.

Jane kept a straight face. 'Yes. A most, a most unfortunate occurrence has, ah – an accident, you see. What happened was . . .'

Mrs Ellen turned round and walked out again, slamming the great oak door behind her. Jane and Guilford looked at each other, across the jagged glass and glistening wine on the table, and giggled. Then they were silent. The silly game did have a meaning, to them.

Jane broke the silence. 'There is one thing we have forgotten.'

'What's that?' he asked.

'A shilling.'

'H'mm?'

'A shilling', Jane said, 'to be really worth a shilling.'

The Privy Council met in the main hall of Northumberland's house at Isleworth, since the Duke now disposed of the English kingdom as though it were a domestic arrangement, with himself as paterfamilias.

'For the love of God,' he adjured the Councillors, 'let us be careful, as men of honour, truth and honesty, that we be ready not only to lay our goods but our lands and lives at the service of this country, and to despise the flattering of ourselves with heaping of riches upon riches.' He told them they had been summoned to hear and countersign King Edward's will, which lay on the table before him. It provided for the Lady Jane Grey to succeed to the throne. They were all to swear on oath that they would support her to the uttermost of their power, and never at any time to swerve from it.

At first there were doubts over the constitutional propriety of proceeding thus. Some of the legalistic lords proposed that a general pardon to all of them be granted under the Great Seal, in case they should hereafter be impeached, by authority of whom they did not specify. Northumberland would not have it. 'I will have no man in better case than myself.'

After a pause Archbishop Cranmer took it upon himself to speak the word that was in every mind. The Act of Parliament granting Henry VIII the right to name his successors had, he pointed out, expired with that

King. If his son wished to exercise the same right, another Act would have to be passed for Parliament to grant it to him. Without that, what they were being asked to approve was, Cranmer said, treason.

There it was. Every eye now watched Northumberland's face in the light of the fine branched candelabra along the table.

'Treason?' he answered, in a deceptively calm voice. 'My Very Reverend Lord of Canterbury, in your hand you are holding the King's will, signed by his royal hand, and you say that to approve of it by adding your own signature might be "treason".'

'My Lord,' – Cranmer was very nervous – 'I merely wished to clarify the –'

He was cut off by the sight of Northumberland rising to his feet, a terrible storm on his brow. '*His will*,' the Duke said. '*What the King has willed*.' His stare travelled all around the table, catching every eye in turn, and he spoke with quiet intensity. 'And you all know full well, my noble Lords, what would befall this kingdom were we' – his voice rose – 'to *disregard*' – quiet again – 'the King's will, do you not, h'm? We shall see his realm returned to Popery. The offices and sacraments and rites of his most holy Church handed back – handed back, as an unlooked-for gift – to the mass-priests and the conjurors of Rome. The kingdom's wealth, my Lords, would not be for all to enjoy, but would be sucked back into the sinks of canting superstition and mystical mumbling still fresh in the memory of every one of us.'

He paused, and enjoyed the perfection of the silence.

Very quietly, he asked, 'Will anyone say "treason" once again?'

Cranmer was gazing at the still flames on the

candelabrum in front of him. He dared not raise his eyes to meet Northumberland's. The Marquess of Winchester shook his head, smiling wanly.

The silence was broken by the scrape of a chair, as the Earl of Arundel stood up. 'My Lords,' Arundel said, 'this document is signed by the King's own hand. I am his loyal subject. I cannot remain among you while there is a question in your minds as to whether his will should be obeyed.'

Arundel quit the room and in doing so precipitated a decision among the rest of the Council. Winchester took the document from in front of Cranmer, signed it, and passed it to Northumberland. He signed it and looked up at Cranmer, who nodded resignedly, took the paper, and added his signature.

As the Councillors took their turn to sign the will, Northumberland said to them, 'My Lords, now that we have settled this question, we should send to the Princesses Mary and Elizabeth to attend upon their brother. He will not be with us on earth for long now.'

In the upper gallery of the hall Sir John Gates had been listening to the Council's proceedings. At Northumberland's words he hastened downstairs. At the same time, Northumberland was leaving the hall to seek Arundel. He saw the Earl at the far end of a passage, talking to a servant of his, who bowed and hurried away as the Duke approached.

'Thank you, my Lord,' Northumberland said.

Arundel stuck out his lower lip, and nodded. 'It had to be said. Alas, alas. How long now?'

'A few days, no more.'

'I see. Well, God rest his soul.'

'Amen,' Northumberland said.

Gates had appeared, clearly impatient to speak with the Duke. Arundel half turned to go, then changed his mind, turned back with a smile and shook the hand of the man who had immured him in the Tower for a year.

Northumberland pressed the Earl's hand firmly, and smiled. In politics, bygones had to be bygones.

Gates watched Arundel depart, and remarked, 'He didn't sign.'

Still smiling, Northumberland shook his head. 'When a chicken is trussed and plucked and lying on your board, you don't need its scratch. Your men are ready?'

'The horses are saddled.'

'Then let them go.'

Gates bowed and hurried away. Northumberland stood there, biting his lip. The game was truly afoot now. He could not have done more than he had to ensure the outcome. All the same, there were hazards. Both princesses were undoubtedly on their guard already. Mary, impulsive Mary, had some days earlier prepared to set out from Essex to visit her dying brother, but had been warned by Sir Nicholas Throckmorton, an old enemy of Northumberland's, that she might never leave London again if she went there now, and she had heeded the advice. Elizabeth, more cannily, had simply sent word that a sickness prevented her from leaving Hatfield. While both of them were at liberty, Northumberland would have to go on biting his lip. He went to find Cranmer,.to instruct him that the customary prayers for the princesses' souls were to be omitted in all churches henceforth.

Gates's armed guards, closely followed by Gates himself, stormed into Mary's house that night. The chief steward was found, pinioned against a wall with a blade at his throat, and told to lead them to where the Princess was. He tried to speak, but fear had dried up his tongue. The house was full of screaming, as maids and servants were manhandled or knocked aside. The steward managed to croak, 'I don't know.' The nick of the blade into his flesh produced no more. 'I don't know.'

Gates had no time to spare. If Mary was alerted she could hide, or escape. He wheeled on a maid who was being held with one arm behind her back, a hand covering her mouth. 'You,' Gates said. 'You will take us to her chambers.'

The maid's eyes, wide with fright, signalled to a passage.

'Bring her,' Gates said, and the maid was frogmarched along the passage. Guards ran on ahead, fanning out through the house.

They passed the ornate chapel, and the maid jabbed a finger to direct them. A door was hurled open, and in the darkness the figure of a woman could be seen, standing with erect dignity, against the moonlit window.

Gates nodded urgently to a lieutenant of the Guards, who stepped forward to the woman. 'Your Grace,' he said, 'we are commanded to arrest you, in the name of . . .' He stopped. Something was wrong. The Princess had not moved a muscle.

Gates drew his sword, walked forward, and prodded the figure. The costumed dummy toppled and fell to the floor.

From all the wings of the house guards returned with nothing to show. Under interrogation, the steward repeatedly vowed that he did not know where the

Princess was, nor had he known that she had left the house. A messenger had called at the house earlier that evening. The horse he had come on was white with lather. He had been shown into the Princess's chambers. That was the last the steward knew of anything.

Gates sat in a high chair, tapping his sword against the knee of his breeches. There was nothing to do. The guards would be billeted here for the night, but tomorrow? The bird could have flown in any direction.

Jane, in a simple woollen gown, was wandering through a copse on a Chiltern hillside. Not since she was a little girl, in the grounds of Bradgate Manor, had she been allowed the freedom to go where she would, as slowly as she wished, alone. It had rained the previous night and now the sunshine of early summertime was drawing the smell of the earth up. A spider's web strung between two bushes lightly covered her face. She brushed it away, with a little thrill that the spider might be crawling upon her. She felt nothing. She took a deep breath, raised her head, and saw birds wheeling in the sky above her. Woodpigeons, she thought.

Guilford was cantering on a bay horse. When he realized that Jane was no longer following him he reined, turned, and scanned the ground he had travelled. 'Jane!' No answer. He felt himself tense up. She might have fallen. 'Jane, where are you?' he called loudly, and heard a faint echo back from the line of trees. He shook the reins and hurried back to look for her.

On the far side of the copse she had come to a slowly flowing river, the bank thick with reeds. Beside it a family of peasants were roasting a skinned rabbit. They looked up, saw the lady come out of the copse, and were terrified.

'Hallo,' Jane said.

But the peasants had already taken to their heels, leaving the rabbit on the fire. They knew the penalties for poaching, even the little children of the family.

'Please,' Jane called after them, 'don't go. I'm not –'

But they had gone, along the river and into the trees.

Guilford had come to the crest of a small rise in the ground. Before him the land fell to a stream, as though embanking it. On the further side of the stream the land rose again, and there he saw Jane's horse, riderless. In alarm he dismounted and ran down to the stream, jumped across it, and stumbled quickly up to the horse. He found that it was neatly tethered to a young elm tree. He called, 'Jane!'

Her voice answered from near by, calmly. 'Come here. See what I have found.'

He smiled to himself, and called back, 'I'll have to tie my horse first,' knowing that the reproach in his voice would have dissipated itself in the thin, sunlit air.

'Come *on*,' Jane called back.

He shrugged, and obeyed. He found her where the stream joined the river. A little skiff, with oars stowed, was moored to a tree. Holding up her gown with one hand, she was clambering into the boat.

'Having won her Lord's heart,' Guilford observed mildly, 'my Lady seeks to stop it.'

She did not hear him, in her excitement. Balanced dangerously in the bobbing skiff, she laughed up at him. 'Come *on*, my love.'

'It isn't strictly ours to use,' he said.

Still laughing for pleasure, beckoning to him, she answered, 'we'll bring it *back*.'

He laughed with her, steadied the boat, got in, and cast off from the mooring. He remembered the last time he had been in a boat, on his way to Dorset Place, and Thomas had tossed his flask of spirits overboard. How quickly and completely one could be altered. The world and the things in it were the same, it was the eyes with which one perceived them that created perspective, and made a new meaning. He took the oars, but needed them only to keep the boat in the stream.

They drifted between tree-lined banks. She trailed a hand in the water. It made scarcely a ripple, stream and boat flowing as one.

'Your father,' she asked, 'what will he want of us?'

'I don't know.' Guilford had that morning received a letter from his father. It ordered him to consummate his marriage. He had told the messenger, solemnly, 'Pray assure my father that I will not fail to obey in what he has commanded me to do.' But it was true that he did not know what future, if any, his father had in mind for them. The marriage was a good one, in social parlance. Perhaps there was no more to it.

'There must be something,' Jane said.

'If so, I don't know it. Why do you ask?'

'Because he frightens me. And I am married to his son.'

'I think . . .' Guilford began, and paused. The fact was that he seldom had thought about the Duke as a public figure, as he must appear in Jane's eyes. It was natural that he wished to be defensive about his father. On the other hand, he had heard gossip in the taverns, had sometimes, at midday, discussed such things with

Thomas and Richard, who had their own sources of opinion, and so he knew that he was the son of a controversial man, without being very clear what the strengths of the arguments were. 'I think', he answered Jane, 'that his deeds are not his nature.'

Her eyes, meeting his, were shaded with scepticism.

'He wanted to *do* something, so he went to Court and became a Councillor.' Guilford grinned impishly, knowing she could recognize her own words.

'But, still . . .'

'Do you know how he came to power?'

'It was when they executed the Protector Somerset.' Jane said.

'Mm. The "Good Duke Somerset". So good, he promised more than he could give. There was an uprising in Norfolk, and my father had to go and put it down.'

'He didn't *have* to.'

'No,' Guilford conceded. 'But he did as he was asked. He always did. Until he lost count of all the men he had locked up in the Tower, tortured, killed. I do not believe my father to be a naturally cruel man. With us he was strict, but not cruel.'

Jane lowered her eyes for a moment. She had never told Guilford the details of how she had been persuaded to marry him. She bitterly resented the memory, even though the outcome was to be drifting with him in a boat, on a summer's day, happier than she'd ever been.

'What my father has done,' Guilford continued, 'was the means he found necessary to achieve the –'

'Necessary? To do what?' Jane interrupted.

'To preserve your Church from what you call the Pit of Popery.'

Jane was shaking her head. 'Guilford,' she said, 'must it always be thus? Are fair ends never to be achieved but by foul means? What is it that . . . Can the strong never be good?'

Guilford had come to the limits of his political experience. Between the private father and public man, Northumberland, he had never been encouraged to make any connections. Perhaps his elder brothers had been. He was not sure. Guilford had always been close to his mother. She had said not a word against her husband, nor a word in explanation of him. 'Who knows?' was the best answer Guilford could give Jane now. He was struck by how wise she seemed to him. That question of hers that had inaugurated this conversation – 'Your father, what will he want of us?' – suddenly began to frighten him, and to depress his spirits. She was right, of course she was. Hitherto his father had never required much of Guilford, beyond the athletic prowess that was native to the family, had never paid serious attention to his third son. But now – Guilford blamed himself as a fool for not having realized it before – the third son had come into the reckoning. 'Love,' he said, 'are you strong enough to go?'

'Go where?' she asked.

'Away.' He leaned forward, across his oars, took her hand, and looked at her yearningly. 'Beyond their reach. It doesn't matter where it is, so long as their touch can't tarnish us. You and me.'

She saw his intensity, saw the fear that lay behind it, and took the question seriously. After some thought, she answered, 'Would that be strong?'

He slumped back helplessly. The boat rocked. 'You see, when I think about your question, I am sure that . . . I just don't believe that our parents will . . .'

'Yes?'

'They won't let us stay like this, Jane, my love.'

Early in July, Henry VIII's 'most precious jewel,' the last Tudor King of England, mumbled 'Lord have mercy on my soul' and expired.

Dr Owen pulled the sheet up over Edward's face, said a quiet prayer, and walked slowly through Greenwich Palace to tell the Duke of Northumberland.

Frances Suffolk had come to see the Duke, and found him very tired and taut. He had slept little for weeks now. The business of administering the State allowed him but a few hours in bed at nights, and those were partly spent in anxious wakefulness. The worst of it, he told Frances, was the endless worrying about the Princesses or, to be particular, about Mary, since Elizabeth was no threat while her sister was at large. After Gates's abortive raid on her house, it was known now that Mary had retreated to Norwich, where she had much support. All this he told Frances in the flat voice of exhaustion, which she, imperious as always, mistook for insouciance.

'Well,' she said, 'surely you must turn back now.' She saw the risk in which she, and her family, stood, and supposed that Northumberland did not care.

'No, madam.' The Duke stroked his forehead with the tips of his fingers. '*Now* we have no choice but to go on.'

'But', Frances interrupted him, 'obviously the Princess knows . . .' She sought to put it delicately, which was not easy for her. 'She must know the design you have concerning the succession, and what that implies to her own position, and . . . So how can you . . .'

'Exactly. Mary knows. And how?' Northumberland's voice took on an acerbity which told Frances that the man still cared as much as ever about his ends.

'Somebody told her,' Frances answered with common sense.

'Yes. Somebody told her who can tell her everything. If she succeeds.'

Frances nodded thoughtfully.

'Our boats are burned, ma'am,' Northumberland was saying. 'There is no turning back –'

It was at that point that Dr Owen entered and, with a bow, reported, 'My Lord. The King is dead.'

Both Frances and Northumberland stood very still. It was she who spoke first, slowly and drily. 'Long live Queen Jane.'

Naked, Jane and Guilford were kneeling on their bed at the Priory, facing each other. Their hands were stretched out to touch each other's. It was a ceremony of innocence they had devised, to make a pledge between them. Among the wonders they had discovered together was that they could be as children again, and not be ashamed of it. She would not have believed that, when she had been deep in her books, corresponding with the Calvinists in Zürich, disputing with Dr Feckenham, taking instruction in Hebrew. She was no less deeply attached to her pursuit of learning now, but her joy in it was richer for the discovery she had made, with Guilford, that the mind need not crouch within the body like a creature hiding in a cave, sheltered from the storm outside, but that mind and body were one organ. 'With my body I thee worship.' It had perplexed her, at their wedding, that phrase in which the Archbishop apparently allowed no distinction between the activity of body and soul. Now she understood it, intuitively. Nor would Guilford, deep in his stews, have believed it possible, this willing and unashamed recovery of childish things. He had not yet come to understand it, in the way that she could, but instinctively he knew that, absurd though the world would have thought them, he did not feel absurd at all. He felt nothing but joy and gratitude for this woman: and fear of losing what they had found.

'So, we will, then,' he said.

'Oh yes,' she responded, 'we will.'

'We will fly.'

'We will fly away.'

'Away, beyond their reach.'

'So far away,' she said, 'that their touch cannot tarnish us.'

'And at last, we will be . . .'

'We will be nothing,' she said, and watched him to see if he understood her. 'Nobody.' Unaccountably she found tears in her eyes. 'Each other's,' she said.

From downstairs, where everyone should have been asleep at the Priory, came the abrupt noise of shouting, and doors being slammed. They stiffened, listening in alarm. Mrs Ellen's voice was plain to hear. She was protesting at something.

Jane and Guilford looked at each other, and quickly started to dress.

Downstairs Mrs Ellen was facing Sir John Gates. Behind him was a detachment of the King's Guard. They had errupted into the house, with shouts for the Lady Jane, until they had aroused the servants, and then the nurse. 'They are asleep,' she told Gates. 'You cannot possibly –'

Gates, seeing that the woman was going to be obstreperous, had decided to ignore her, and gave the nod to search the house until the Lady Jane had been found. Whereupon Mrs Ellen had barred the way up the staircase, a defence that would not have lasted long had not Jane and Guilford, with clothes loosely pulled on, then appeared at the top of the staircase and come down.

Immediately the guardsmen stood where they were and drew back their shoulders in respectful attention. Gates stepped forward to meet Jane at the foot of the stairs. 'My Lady Jane.'

'Who calls for her?' Jane demanded.

Gates made a small bow. 'You must now come with us, ma'am.'

Her lips parted, and her face turned pale. 'Who sent you?'

# III

The doors to the throne room at Whitehall Palace were opened, to admit Jane, dressed in a robe of red velvet, with a line of gilt buttons that ran down the bodice and the length of the full skirt. She was followed by Guilford, Mrs Ellen, and Gates. At the far end of the cloistered room stood the throne, empty, on a carpeted dais. At one side of it stood Northumberland and Winchester, the Lord Chancellor, at the other side Frances and Henry Suffolk, and John and Robert Dudley, waiting. Along each side of the room were arrayed the Privy Councillors, in their most superb trappings. As the doors were closed behind her, Jane saw everyone bow or curtsy to her. She was utterly bewildered, and blushed with embarrassment. It was a joke, a gross mistake, a nightmare. It could not be any such thing. Her brain was too numbed to comprehend the only thing that could be going on. Everyone was behaving as though the King was there. But Edward was nowhere to be seen. She stood still, waiting to see what would happen. Guilford was just behind her. Without him, she thought she would have fainted with terror.

Northumberland took two paces forward. 'My Lords,' he said, 'as President of the Council I must, with infinite regret, announce the death of His most blessed and gracious Majesty King Edward the Sixth.'

Jane was quite unprepared for the news. No more than the rest of the English people had she suspected that the King's illness would prove mortal so swiftly. As yet she was too stunned and confused to grieve for her dear friend. She closed her eyes. Mrs Ellen moved to her elbow, seeing Jane sway with the shock.

Northumberland was expatiating upon the deep sorrow he felt, which he knew would be shared by a grieving nation. But he bade all to take comfort from the virtuous life the King had led, to rejoice in the prudence and goodness of Edward's reign, and give thanks for the care he had taken to keep the realm safe from the intrigues and blandishments of Rome. 'At the close of his life he was praying God to defend England from the Popish faith, and to deliver it from the rule of his evil sisters.'

Northumberland paused, as though renewing his strength for the weighty words he had to say, but in fact running his eyes over all who were there to ascertain their responses. They seemed favourable, he thought. Councillors were nodding their heads sagely, and whispering with approval to their neighbours. The small figure of Jane stood quite still, her face pallid. Guilford's brothers were moving very discreetly down the hall. They came to stand close to Guilford, one each side of him, hemming him in.

Northumberland had picked up a paper. Despite himself, he could not prevent his hands from shaking slightly as he read from it. His voice was harsh with nervousness. 'Shortly before his death, His Majesty made a declaration, which has been witnessed by his Council, and marked with his Great Seal. In it, he stated that it was his will that whosoever should acknowledge the Lady Mary or the Lady Elizabeth as heirs to the crown should be judged as traitors.'

Northumberland paused again, and in the silence Jane felt herself start to tremble. Intuition, if not reason, knew what was coming.

'My Lady,' Northumberland continued, looking at Jane, 'His Majesty named your Grace heir to his crown.'

All eyes turned to look at her. For many of those present, it was the first time they had seen her. She saw the lines of faces, some hard, some triumphant, examining her.

Northumberland was saying, 'There but remains for your Grace gratefully to accept the high estate which God Almighty, who disposes of all crowns and sceptres and is never sufficiently to be thanked by you, hath advanced you to.'

He waited for some words from her, but was not disconcerted when none were spoken. It was understandable that she should feel overwhelmed at the present juncture. She was very young. Though still shaking with the significance of the moment, he felt confident of guiding her through the ceremony.

'Long live Queen Jane!' he shouted.

The Councillors responded, 'Long live Queen Jane!'

Her lips were moving very slowly, saying, without sound, 'Queen Jane?'

Frances and Henry had come towards their daughter, curtsied and bowed to her, and now began to walk backwards, before her, towards the throne.

'From us,' Northumberland said, 'receive first the humble duty, tendered to you upon our knees, which shortly shall be paid to you by all your kingdom.'

The company prepared to kneel, but Jane had not moved. She had offered up a silent prayer for divine guidance in what she should now do. She was waiting for enlightenment.

Frances hissed, 'Walk, Jane.'

For the first time Jane spoke. 'I cannot. I will not.'

'Jane. *Walk*.' Franced glared at her, and resumed her backward progress towards the empty throne.

With a desperate look back at Guilford, who was prevented from moving by his brothers, Jane walked up the room to the throne. As she passed, the Councillors sank to their knees. Northumberland was the last to do so, as she stepped onto the dais. He bowed his head, then raised it again, and his eyes met hers. She thought she was looking at the gates of hell. She swayed, stumbled, and broke into sobs.

Everyone waited. It was not untoward. They were all grieving at the death of their boy King, and it was fitting that one so young should give vent to tears.

The Marquess of Winchester kissed her hand, stood up, and took the imperial crown from a cushion borne by a servant. The Black Prince's ruby and Edward the Confessor's sapphire gleamed at her from the diadem surrounding a velvet cap, all surmounted by orb and cross. At the sight of the cross her tears stopped, dried up by appalling fear of what they all wanted her to do. No head should wear the crown save one whom God had appointed as His deputy on earth. If she colluded with these implacable faces that hedged her in, she would commit a blasphemy.

Quietly, Winchester asked, 'Your Majesty will try the crown?' He raised it towards her head.

She recoiled. 'This is not mine. It pleases me not.'

Northumberland stood up, towering over her tiny figure. 'It is yours, your Grace, by the late King's will.'

'It is not my right.'

In a reasonable voice, as though he were a tutor correcting her, Northumberland asked, 'Then whose right is it?'

Jane's mouth opened, but 'I –' was all she could say.

Winchester, still holding the crown upraised, murmured, 'Your Grace will wish to see that it fits.'

'I don't – I can't –'

Frances growled, 'Let us see if it fits Your Majesty's head.'

Jane did not know what to do. God had not answered her prayer. To obey's one's parents was pleasing in the sight of God. Northumberland was a giant beside her. She trembled, and remained still while Winchester put the crown on her head.

It slipped down a little on one side, but Frances's hand was there to straighten it.

'It does fit Your Majesty,' Winchester declared, as pleased as a milliner.

'So it does!' Northumberland concurred.

And everyone suddenly burst out clapping, led by Northumberland. Under the applause, Winchester whispered kindly to Jane, 'And now another shall be made.'

'Another?' Jane asked, bemused. 'Why?'

'Why?' Winchester echoed. 'To crown your husband's head as well.'

The ghastly absurdity of it cracked the panic in which she had been frozen. 'Oh, *Guilford!*' she screamed, and tore the crown from her head.

All noise died to silence. Then the pattering of her feet was heard, as she darted through the knot of people around her and ran down the room, away from the throne. Guilford saw her coming, pushed his brothers away from him, and ran to meet her.

Beside the throne, Northumberland had raised a hand to dissuade Frances and Henry from chasing after their daughter. That would only make things worse.

In the middle of the room, regardless of being watched by the whole company of Councillors and nobility, Jane seized Guilford's hands and begged him, 'Oh my love, please, take me out of here. Away. Beyond their reach.'

Guilford glanced at the Councillors. 'They say that you are the Queen.'

Surely Guilford wasn't betraying her? With an edge of despair on her voice, she asked him, 'What are you saying?'

He saw her fear, and assuaged it, squeezing her hands, and smiling almost mischievously. 'I am saying only what they say,' he replied, then turned to address the company. 'My Lords. The Queen desires that you withdraw.'

Again, for a few seconds, the room, full of people, was intensely silent, as though the entire crew had frozen to death. Frances's face wore a black scowl. The impudence of the girl. And again it was Northumberland, his nerves exhausted but his judgement still swift, who gave others their part to play. Decisively he bowed to Jane and walked through an arch into the cloister that ran round the room. The rest of the company followed suit. All remained behind the arches, in knots of whispering and watching and waiting.

Jane and Guilford were alone, in the centre of the room.

'Wake me,' she pleaded.

'My love . . .' Guilford spoke tenderly, but with the faintest hint of reproach in his voice. From outside the cruel centre of the event, he had already assessed that there was no escaping it, and had started to take the best view that he could.

'This is a nightmare,' Jane sobbed. 'Wake me.'

'Jane . . .'

'He wants to make you King.'

That set Guilford aback. He looked at her in disbelief. 'Who does?'

'Your father. This is what he wants. I saw his face. For you to be his puppet. And me yours.'

'I didn't . . .' Guilford paused. 'I had no idea.'

'You swear?'

Guilford's mouth tensed angrily. Did she think that all their time at the Priory had been so much dissembling on his part? That he was in league with his father? That he would want to be King, any more than she to be Queen? 'Of course I swear it,' he threw back at her. 'What do you take me for?'

'Oh.' Jane's eyes closed, and her body swayed. In a little voice, she asked, 'What am I to do?'

Guilford took her by the shoulders. 'Jane. You said once, that if I felt the commonwealth was sick, then I should seek to cure it.'

'Yes.' Her eyes opened again at Guilford's persuasive tone of voice.

'By coming to Court, you said. Becoming a Councillor. *Doing* something.'

'Yes. But then you said, there is nothing to be done. Nothing would have any effect. And you said, let's fly away . . .'

'My love,' Guilford told her, 'before we met, you and I, I could feel – oh, feel things deeply. But I did not think. You – you thought, you studied –'

Jane shook her head. He was trying to reconcile her, and she wanted to resist that as much as she had wanted to resist his father. 'Yes,' she answered, impatiently, 'I know, but –'

'Jane.' He held her shoulders firmly. 'We are like a coin. With a head on one side, and on the other a lion, heart of England . . . And either side, on its own, is worth nothing. But, together, you and I, we might . . . we *might* find that it's possible to stay untarnished. That the strong can yet be good.' She was avoiding his eyes. He held her tight, and waited until she looked at him, and then told her, 'I couldn't care less if I am King. But I want you to be Queen.'

He held her by the hand, and took a step towards the throne. She followed, as though she were docile. Step by step he led her to the dais, then handed her on in front of him, and sat her on the throne.

With a smile he looked up at her, and asked, 'Now, my love, was that so hard?'

Behind the arches the people who had been watching now glanced at each other and returned to the main floor. Guilford remained beside his wife, standing with his feet slightly apart, and head erect, looking down the length of the room.

When the shuffling and the murmuring had subsided, and all the company were gathered in front of her again, quiet, Jane stood up. 'My Lord Northumberland.'

The Duke stepped forward and knelt before her. 'Your Grace?'

'You have told us that we are Queen.'

'By the will of your late cous –'

She cut him off. 'We may issue our commands, and it is your sworn duty to obey them?'

Northumberland's eyes looked up at her, guardedly. 'Yes, of course, Your Majesty.'

'Well, then,' said the Queen. 'We want . . .' She hesitated, as the fear and tension took its toll of her. Confronted by the noble class of England, she was a little girl, a tear running down her cheek. Her voice lost its crispness, and wavered. 'I want a real shilling,' she said.

The liveried boatmen dipped and hauled, dipped and hauled, and as the procession of carved and canopied barges moved down the Thames the sunlight flashed on their feathering blades, and on the jewels and bright stuffs of the royal party and accompanying nobility. Jane, in the leading barge, had been dressed in green and white, the bodice shot through with thread of gold. Her coif was studded with brilliant gems and pearls. Beside her the blond figure of Guilford was no less resplendent in white and gold. To those watching from the river bank the procession was a scintillating emblem of majesty, but no one cheered or waved. The people watched in a dull, resentful silence.

When the leading barge came into the view of those waiting at the Tower, a cannon was fired. The gunpowder smoke hung wreathed in the still summer air before slowly drifting away. The ravens were briefly startled. The cannon sounded again as Queen Jane disembarked, and crossed the drawbridge into Tower Green, passing the hideous heads on Traitors' Gate.

The Lieutenant of the Tower, Sir John Bridges, was waiting with the keys he had to present to the new monarch. He knelt as Jane approached. From behind her, Northumberland hastened his pace and took the keys from Bridges first, then turned, knelt, and presented them himself. A third cannon shot was fired.

Bridges conducted the party across the Green to the White Tower and the royal lodgings. Bounding the Tower were the keeps, where important prisoners languished. Facing it, across the Green, was the Mint. The rest of the quadrangle was composed of small houses, barracks, stables and smithies, with courtyards behind them. Beyond were the battlements and Tower Hill, overlooking the huddled city, the river, and broad green meadows. The flags hung limp. At doorways and windows people stood in silence watching Jane cross the Green. Servants bowed or curtsied, but the only loyal cheers came from those who had been bribed to it.

The party ascended to the battlements, where a stool had been set for the Queen to stand on, so that her diminutive figure should appear royally. Behind her Guilford, the Dudleys and Suffolks, Bridges, noblemen and Councillors ranged themselves to face the crowd that had gathered below in the fields. Trumpets fanfared, and a herald stepped forward. 'Know ye', he announced, 'that by the grace of God, and the will of His late servant Edward, of the most blessed memory, be proclaimed Jane Queen of England, Ireland, and France . . .'

A score of men uttered loud huzzahs and were moved

to throw their caps in the air. The other hundreds of listening people were not visibly moved at all. Only that morning had they heard of the death of their King, and for him they grieved, but the faces they presented to his successor were sullen.

The herald continued, '. . . with all the royalties and pre-eminences to the same belonging, Defender of the Faith, Supreme Head of the Church . . .'

Those phrases stirred Jane, for all her reluctance to be where she found herself. In what time she had had to gather her wits, to possess herself again, she had taken courage from the thought that she would be able to uphold and pursue the reformation of the people's religion, the work for which she had most admired Edward. If she had strength at all to go on, it would be from her faith. A few hours previously, looking into Northumberland's eyes beside the throne, she would not have believed even that possible.

After the proclamation, Jane and Guilford were conducted to their apartments in the Tower. Mrs Ellen was there to greet them. The first thing Jane did, in that sumptuous room, was to fling herself on the bed, sobbing broken-heartedly.

Guilford was quickly at her side. 'Now, what's the matter?' he asked. He had thought until now that she had reconciled herself. On the barge she had looked quite proud, her head held erect, looking down the river towards the Tower, the breeze of the boat's passage lightly fluttering her fine costume. He had thought that perhaps the worst was over. What remained might be a long struggle with his father, but no more crises. So there was a trace of irritation as he asked his weeping wife, 'What's the matter?'

'What do you think is the matter?' she answered. 'He's dead. The only person who was dear to me.'

Guilford frowned, and nodded. 'Of course. I am sorry.'

He held her, and her sobbing subsided. She sensed that she had upset him. Looking into his face, she added, 'Except – I mean, until . . .'

He took her hands and shook his head with a wry smile. She did not have to say it.

Her face became nearly wistful. 'They didn't cheer,' she observed. 'Only some of the soldiers, and your father's men. The people were not cheering at all.'

'They will,' he reassured her. 'You'll see.'

As they spoke, in the districts of London heralds were again proclaiming Jane the rightful queen, and calling the people to repel the feigned claim of the Lady Mary, bastard daughter of King Henry VIII, of famous memory. The people listened with one ear, and most of them showed no response. A few grieved for dead King Edward. A few others muttered that Mary's claim was the better one, and that she was being robbed of her rightful inheritance by the villainous Duke of Northumberland. Some said so openly, in the hearing of the constables. One man who did so was pilloried, with his ears nailed to the wooden board, and when he was released his ears were severed from his head, and remained nailed on the pillory, to remind all others of like mind.

Northumberland came into the Council Chamber with a letter. Among the Privy Councillors, seated around a candlelit table, Henry Suffolk and Sir John Gates clapped his entry. Northumberland silenced them briskly with a little flap of the letter. It was from Princess Mary at Framlingham Castle, and advised the Council to avert bloodshed by honouring her claim to the throne, promising respect for the reformed faith, but all Northumberland said was, 'Mary has proclaimed herself Queen.' He knew, as he always did, what had to be done, and all he wanted from the Council was their help in doing it, not their long-winded and pusillanimous observations on the fine points of the constitutional position.

'Well,' Henry said as Northumberland was taking his seat at the head of the table, 'there's no great surprise.'

'Indeed not,' replied Northumberland, running his eyes over the Councillors' faces. 'But it does require an answer.'

Winchester nodded. 'I am sure, my Lord, that we can this evening expediently draft a letter in reply in which we . . .'

'No,' Northumberland interrupted him. 'I do not mean to answer with a letter, but with an army.' He turned to Suffolk. 'Henry, how quickly could you raise a force?'

Suffolk, pleased with the appointment, answered, 'It would depend on how large the force is to be.'

'Well,' rejoined Northumberland, 'say two thousand horse? Three thousand foot? Artillery?'

At that some breaths were drawn, some heads turned to see how the others were taking it. While Suffolk was considering the question it was the Earl of Arundel who observed, 'My Lord, that does seem . . . To arrest one woman, with a dubious title to the throne, that does seem, ah, a very *large* . . .'

Northumberland was not even looking at the Earl, but

at Suffolk, waiting for the answer to the question that mattered.

'Three days?' Suffolk proposed.

In St Luke's Gospel Jane had found the passage she was looking for. She began to read it out loud to Guilford, who smiled blankly at her. She smiled back, and translated from the Greek. 'And there was delivered unto him the book of the prophet Esaias. And when he had opened the book, he found the place where it was written. The spirit of the Lord God is upon me, because he hath anointed me to preach the gospel to the poor; he hath sent me to heal the brokenhearted, to preach deliverance to the captives, and recovering of sight to the blind, to set at liberty them that are bruised.' She shut the book, and looked enquiringly at Guilford.

'Why not?' he said. Already, on the other side of Tower Green, pure silver was being melted and moulded for shillings. When the Queen spoke, it was for her subjects to obey.

He went with her. Sir John Bridges was not at all happy about what Her Majesty commanded him to do, but he could not refuse, unless he wished to take the place of those she released. Walking along the corridor of prison cells, he read aloud from a list he had. 'Sir Thomas Holcroft, arrested with the Duke of Somerset for treason –'

'Yes,' the Queen said, 'yes, release him. Go on.'

'The Mayor of Norwich, ma'am. Incarcerated by order of my Lord Northumb –'

'Of course. Release him. And anybody who –'

Before he unlocked, Bridges felt he had to make a last

effort to make the Queen understand how matters really stood. He would have to answer to the Lord Protector for acquiescing in this madness. 'Now, your Grace,' he began, 'I must with all respect –'

Jane spoke coolly. 'Now, Guilford, please would you take the Lieutenant's keys from him.'

Bridges avoided the indignity. He unlocked a cell door, opened it slowly and addressed those within. 'Masters, you are free men.' He swallowed. 'By express order of Her Majesty, Queen Jane.'

Two prisoners, in the shabby remnants of what had once been fine costumes, their heads bald in patches with lice, emerged suspiciously. When they saw Jane, they knew who she must be. They were as well informed, by their goalers, as any citizens of what had been doing outside these stone walls. They bowed low and crept swiftly away.

Jane smiled sweetly at Bridges, suppressing an impulse to say, 'Now, my love, was that so hard?'

Bridges coughed. 'And now, ma'am, I should remind your Grace that his Excellency the Spanish Ambassador is –'

'Tomorrow!' she cried, and strode on towards the next cell door.

The Marquess of Winchester was also given cause for thought about the new Queen's intentions. Descending a staircase in the White Tower, he heard a commotion from the other end of a passageway and went to look into it. He found a procession of maids winding down a spiral staircase that led from the royal apartments. They were carrying piles of gowns, kirtles, bodices, furs, lengths of velvet and silk not yet made up, stockings, shoes, and gloves. Directing them was a housekeeper in a towering rage.

'Mistress,' Winchester asked her, 'what is this?'

'Ah, my Lord,' she answered, in a more vexed voice than she would normally have used to the nobility, 'this, my good Lord, is the royal wardrobe, do you see?'

'Yes,' Winchester said. 'But why –'

'Why, my Lord, why?' The housekeeper fanned her brow with her hand. 'Because the Queen is giving it away.'

'The Queen is – what did you say, mistress?'

'Giving it away, my Lord.' The housekeeper's voice sarcastically imitated Jane's. ' "To warm the wretched and to clothe the comfortless." Thus she said. "All, all away." Ay, I never thought to serve a queen who wore the imperial crown and now, I tell you truth, my Lord, I do not know how I shall manage in it.'

Winchester watched the housekeeper followed her burdened maids, shaking her head and clucking her tongue as she went.

Across the Green the Master of the Mint took a mallet and banged the inverted moulds. Glittering shillings showered down.

The Ambassador from His Imperial Majesty Charles V of Spain, Holy Roman Emperor, was Simon Renard. Twice now had he waited upon the new Queen of England, and twice failed to gain an audience of her. The third time he was admitted, to find Jane and Guilford informally dressed, seated at a table, and working so hard together at the preparation of a document that they scarcely glanced up at him. He maintained the protocol, the bowed knee and the flourished hat, nevertheless. If Her Majesty saw fit to treat the envoy of the most powerful man in Europe as though he were a tinker, let that be a reflection upon her. She was extraordinarily young, much more so in appearance than her cousin, the late King, even though it was said they were exactly of an age. Her husband was a drunken buffoon, he had heard, and the boy's demeanour now, not rising to his feet, even though he had not the excuse that Her Majesty had – the frailty of the fair sex – corroborated the reports.

'Your Grace,' Renard said.

'Your Excellency,' Jane replied, with an offhand nod. 'We regret that we have only a moment to spare for whatever business it is that brings you to see us.'

'Your Grace,' said Renard, with dignified reproach, 'I have several times –'

'Indeed.' Jane was leaning over the document on the table before her, emending some words. 'We have had more pressing matters upon our attention.'

'Why, of course, your Grace.' He wondered what matters could be more pressing to an English monarch than relations with the country to whose pipe the rest of Europe jigged, but he would make allowances for her inexperience. With another sweep of his feathered hat, he said, 'I bring the humblest salutations from –'

She interrupted him. 'Matters that are even more pressing than the fawning blandishments of the King of Spain.'

Renard managed a frozen smile. 'Yes. Yes, I see.' What he saw, as he bowed and left, was that he would have to tell Northumberland to speak very sharply indeed to this little creature he had elevated.

The document on which Jane and Guilford were working went with them, later that evening, to a meeting of the Privy Council. As they entered the chamber Jane saw that Northumberland, too, had a document before him on the table. Nervous about what she had to do, she was holding her papers so tightly that the edge was crumpled. 'My Lords,' she greeted the Councillors.

They rose to their feet with a murmur of 'your Grace'.

She wanted to turn and flee from them. From behind, Guilford gave her an encouraging little push in the back. She walked quickly to the throne of the Council, sat down, and called them to order. 'My Lords.'

Eyebrows were raised. What did the girl think she was playing at?

Jane waited until they had all sat down again, and then read from the document she held. 'These are the things we command you to see are done. Item . . .' Her eyes flickered to Guilford, who sent back a little smile of encouragement. She went on, 'We wish, first, for you to call a Parliament, to repeal the laws relating to the branding of those unfortunates forced into beggary.'

Some of the Councillors' mouths had opened in amazement. This was not what the meeting had been called for. Anxious glances were cast in the direction of the Duke of Northumberland. It seemed that he had done nothing to prepare her for her part in the Council's meetings. He would have to do something now, quickly. There was no time for earnest, childish pratings about goodwill to all men, and certainly no taste for it among the Councillors.

'Instead,' Jane continued, 'we command, second, that all those lands and properties which our great-uncle

King Henry did sequestrate from the Popish monasteries be returned for the use and cultivation of the common people, in perpetuity.'

Northumberland, seated at Jane's right hand, did not look perturbed. He sat with his chin resting on his folded hands, studying his own document, apparently content to let the child chatter on for as long as it pleased her to do so.

Jane cleared her throat, looked to Guilford for further reassurance, and articulated their third command. 'We wish that a school be endowed. It will be for teaching the children of the poor, not by beating or cajolement, but by tender affection and nurture. It will be named for the memory of our cousin Edward, and its founding we put in our father's care. He shall commence this stewardship forthwith. Item . . .'

So slowly that it might have been with apology, Northumberland had turned the document before him around, so that it lay before the Queen.

She saw what he had done, and asked, 'What is this?'

'It concerns your father, ma'am. It is your commission to him to lead your army into Norfolk, to repel the traitor, the Lady Mary.'

Jane felt her throat dry. Her body, which had gathered some self-confidence from speaking, was immediately drained of energy. A sagging, limp figure in the great throne at the head of the table, she shook her head in confusion. 'H'm?' was all she found to say. She looked to Guilford for assistance. His face conveyed dismay, nothing more.

She would not put her signature to the commission then and there. She told the Council she had need of retiring, to consider well what she would do. That was the truth; for, in the space of three days, she had already learned that she could fight back against these people, given time to refresh her spirit after each blow such as this one. She had the gift, moreover, of concentrating her mind on what the moment required. It was easy for her to postpone the charter of commands that she had drawn up with Guilford. As though it were a difficult passage in Plato, she now wrestled with the problem that her father-in-law had placed before her.

So it was that by the time she had reached a small state room, where Guilford, Northumberland, and her parents joined her, her temper was up again.

Her father started to remonstrate with her. 'Jane, this decision was unanimous –'

'Decision?' she interrupted, and waved the commission at him. 'This is no decision.'

'But your Grace,' Northumberland corrected her, 'be assured that the whole Council considered the matter for many a –'

Again she interrupted. 'It is not "the" Council, my Lord. It is *our* Council, our Privy Council. And our Council has not at all considered what feelings we might have in the matter.'

Since that was clearly true, no one contradicted her.

She looked at Suffolk. 'You, sir, are our father. We have important work for you to do, as you have heard.' She did not add that, ineffectual and acquiescent as he was, he was the sole member of the Council who might, in an extremity, perhaps have some personal sympathy for her. It was small comfort, but better that than to be left at the cold mercy of the Protector. She threw her head back, and thrust out her chin. Looking Northumberland in the eyes, she told him, 'We would like our father . . . We demand that he tarry with us. For we have need of him.'

Suffolk was quite taken aback by his daughter's vehemence. 'Jane,' he said, and there was sincere concern in his voice, 'Jane, you see, now, unless we –'

His wife's voice overrode him. 'This is absurd,' she pronounced. She might be excluded, as a woman, from the Privy Council, but she knew herself to be as formidable and well informed as any of them. 'Who else', she demanded, 'do you propose should lead –'

But she in turn was interrupted by Guilford, who blurted out, 'Jane, I told you that my father is an honest man.' He felt Northumberland's eyes upon him, but did not look back.

'Yes?' Jane said.

'So let him prove it to you. Send him to defend your throne. Ask *him*.'

In the silence that followed Guilford's proposal, he could not forbear from seeing how his father had received it. Northumberland's face was impassive.

Jane held the commission out to him. 'My Lord,' she said. 'I will sign this document if the words "our father Henry, Duke of Suffolk" be struck out, and in their place be put "our well beloved and trusted Councillor John, Duke of Northumberland".'

Frances snorted and was about to dismiss the idea when Northumberland took the commission from Jane's hands, went to a writing trable, and dipped a quill in the inkpot. His brain, so well used now to calculating policy, had already summed up his son's proposal. He was hated everywhere, about which he cared not at all, but he was especially hated in Norfolk, after his brutal suppression of the uprising there. He disliked the proposal for another, stronger reason, too. He could not trust the Privy Council to reach right decisions in his absence, nor trust his enemies there not to have him supplanted. On the other hand, he reckoned, he was the best leader of men in England, and was far more likely than Henry Suffolk to bring the thing to a speedy and successful conclusion. And, the final and most weighty argument of all, this little girl whom he had set upon the throne was worrying him as a terrier worries a boar. She was the Queen, and she had to be obeyed. Later, when Mary had been dealt with, he would use experience and flattery, as he had upon Edward, to mould her more suitably. For the present, expediency was all. He made the changes she had requested in the commission and handed it back to her, with the quill. He bowed. 'I am your servant, ma'am.'

Astonished by the man's compliance, and a little frightened at her successful exercise of the power he had wished upon her, she signed the document carefully, lest her hand shake. She handed it to him, and almost stuttered, 'Then we . . . we wish you God-speed, my Lord.'

Northumberland had taken the commission and was turning to leave when Frances, enraged to have been opposed and thwarted by a daughter she could have thrashed into submission, decided to taunt Northumberland for, as she saw it, betraying her. ' "I can . . ." ' she started to say, then thought better of it.

Northumberland turned slowly upon her, and searched her with his icy blue eyes. 'My Lady?'

Frances set her mouth, and threw the words back at

him. ' "I can control him. He can be controlled . . ." '

The Duke paused, then gave the Duchess an ironic little bow, and left quickly.

Jane was puzzled. 'What did you mean by that?' she asked her mother.

Frances glowered. 'I mean . . . you stupid girl. You foolish, wilful little girl.'

Jane remained poised. Having seen the Protector bend to her will, she would not be tyrannized by a woman for whom she felt intimate hatred. 'Mother, I would have thought the Duke a most proper choice for the commission, with the experience he already has of putting down revolts among those people of Norfolk.'

'Yes,' replied Frances, smiling bitterly with anger, and with the sense she had that this reckless and ungrateful child of hers was going to destroy everything. 'Precisely. But, after all,' she added, leaving the room, ' "We are the Queen".'

Jane looked at her father for enlightenment. None came. What was happening had gone beyond Henry's power of understanding. He offered his daughter a wan smile.

Northumberland had gone back into the adjourned Council meeting. Calmly, firmly, he was saying, 'I would remind all of you who it was put that young girl on the throne. I would remind all of you that she is here because of our insistence, not at her own request.' He paused. 'Nor at her own wish.' With the commission in his hand, he prepared to leave.

Winchester spoke up. 'My Lord, you need not distrust us. We know, all of us, that we are as implicated in this matter as you are. We can none of us wipe our hands clean of it.'

He was answered with a long look in the eyes, of which the meaning was plain: Look to it that you mean what you say, or be ready to answer to me with your life.

When Northumberland had left the chamber the Earl of Arundel coughed several times. Winchester turned to him, to see what was wrong. Arundel dismissed it with a wave of the hand. Just a tickle in the throat.

The next morning Northumberland mounted his horse outside the White Tower, to set off for Norfolk. With him were his sons John and Robert, Gates, and the lieutenants of the military expedition. In burnished armour, a red cloak flowing from his shoulders, Northumberland addressed the Councillors, gathered to wish him God-speed. Jane and Guilford watched from a window of their royal apartments. The sun shone splendidly on the ancient stones, the lawns, cupolas and flags, glinting on breastplate and brass buckle.

'We are going to hazard our lives for all your sakes, as for the Queen's Majesty,' Northumberland said. 'Our properties, goods, and families we entrust to your safe keeping. Had we thought that any one among you, in the hope of life and preferment, would conspire to betray us, and leave us in the briars, we could have provided otherwise. But we think we are assured of your fidelities, the violation of which would be revenged by Almighty God most surely and dreadfully.'

The Duke's heels nudged his horse, and the party clattered away to meet up with the army. In the streets of London, and indeed later on in Middlesex and Hertfordshire, he could not fail to notice that not one citizen raised his hat or bade them God-speed. Though many must be of the reformed faith, their attachment to that was less devout than their hatred of the Duke of Northumberland.

Arundel and Winchester watched him leave the Tower, then caught each other's eye. Arundel coughed.

'Are you unwell, my Lord?' Winchester asked.

'No, no,' Arundel answered. 'It is that . . . I like not the air.' He moved away, preoccupied. Where should a prudent man repose his trust? Suppose that Northumberland, arriving in Norfolk, found an opposing force too great to combat: would the Duke go over to the Lady Mary's cause? If so, would it then be held treasonable to have remained loyal to the cause he had left behind? Other eventualities could be imagined, and it was very hard to know where a man might find a firm footing.

Jane, meanwhile, had been presented with a purse sent across from the Mint. She opened it curiously and took out one of the brilliant silver coins inside. It bore a profile of her head. She turned in delight to Guilford, and showed him a shilling worth a shilling.

The Privy Council was in virtually constant session for two days, late into the nights. The news that was brought back to them was never good for those, hourly diminishing in number, who continued to profess loyalty to Queen Jane. The Earl of Bath had sent his sons and tenants to join the Princess Mary's forces. The Earls of Mordaunt and Wharton had done likewise. Ships stationed at Yarmouth, to prevent Mary from escaping abroad, had gone over to her side. The East Anglian peasants, though mostly Protestant, had taken up arms for her. She had been proclaimed Queen in Derby, Devonshire, Oxford.

'And what news of our force?' the Duke of Suffolk asked.

Winchester shrugged, and gazed in silence down the long Council table, where several seats were vacant. The Earl of Arundel uttered his little dry cough.

The answer to Suffolk's question arrived a few hours later that night. At the Great Door of the Tower a loud and prolonged banging was answered by a porter. 'Who's there?' he called.

'Robert Dudley,' a voice called back.

The porter checked through his peep-hole, and opened the door. Robert Dudley was slumped forward on his horse's neck, exhausted. He was attended by a handful of soldiers on foot. They were all grimy with travel. The horse stumbled as it entered, and Robert slithered off. The soldiers broke his fall for him.

To the porter he said, 'Take me to my brother.'

Sending a servant ahead to wake Guilford, the porter helped Robert to get across the courtyard and into the White Tower. Guilford, hastily dressed in a shirt, met him on the staircase.

Robert sat down there, his elbows on his knees and his head in his hands. 'Desertions,' he told Guilford. 'In their hundreds. Overnight. They melt away.' He sighed, and massaged his eyes wearily.

Guilford sat down beside him. 'And our father?'

Robert shook his head, very slowly. 'I don't know. It's hopeless. We doubled their wages, and still they vanish. In the morning you see a score remaining of the hundred men who lay down to sleep. And none join us. You could double the wages again, and it would be the same. They desert, go home, some go over to the papists. And even those that stay are brawling with each other. It's all up for us, Guilford, unless the Council send fresh forces at once. Enlisted men. Or else we are lost.'

Guilford stood, and held out his hand. 'Come,' he said, 'let us go and tell the Council now. They are in the chamber.'

Robert looked up at his brother, but did not take his hand. He was too tired to stand. He slumped back onto his elbows, and his sword clattered against the stone stairs. 'It was so foolish, Guilford. Whoever thought that *he* should lead a force to Norfolk?' He shook his head again. 'Norfolk. They all hate him, the people there.' And he laughed, too bone weary to dodge the ironies any longer.

Guilford left him there, and hurried up to find Jane. She was sitting up in bed, reading. 'Jane,' he said, urgently, 'come with me.'

'H'm?' Where to?'

'The Council Chamber.'

'But I'm –' she answered. 'I must get dressed first.'

Guilford found a long, loose gown and threw it to her. 'Love, there is no need. Come now.'

The great vault of the chamber still glowed with candlelight, but nobody was there. The chairs remained where the Councillors had pushed them back to depart, impelled by the latest news from Norfolk. In the morning servants would come in to straighten the chairs and renew the candles.

Jane and Guilford, in their loose shifts, surveyed the empty space. 'All gone,' Guilford said quietly.

'All those mighty Lords and Bishops,' she observed, 'with their solemn pledge to serve me even unto death . . . Nine days, was it?'

'You should have kept Sir John Bridges' keys.' Guilford made the joke gentle. It had all happened so quickly he was not sure whether she understood how grave their position was, still less how dark the future seemed. From the Council she had heard about the military reverses, but apparently regarded them as setbacks for Northumberland, of no great consequence to herself. Now she was wandering around the long table, with the air of being amused to find a vacancy where there had been men of such weighty deliberation.

She leaned and blew out a candle, and laughed quietly. 'So now we are really on our own. Now we are really ruling England.' She blew out another candle.

Guilford decided that it was not the moment to point out that exactly the reverse was likely to be the outcome. Instead, he played their game. 'So,' he asked, 'what do you want?'

'I want . . .' She reflected. 'No brandings for the famished. Contentment and comfort in the country. Peace.'

Guilford blew out a candle. 'It's done. I want . . . your country to remain true to your faith. No popes or cardinals. No parents who abuse their children.'

Jane blew out a candle. 'Then it's done.' One candle still burned, in the room otherwise lit by torches in brackets on the walls. 'I want . . .' She paused, then impulsively snuffed out the last candle with her fingers. 'Oh, I want this to be over.'

'Done,' said a voice from the other end of the room. Her father had entered, looking for her. Mrs Ellen was with him.

Henry strode to the throne and with two hands ripped off the back of the canopy, with the royal crest upon it.

He tossed it aside and walked towards his daughter. 'The Council has just met in Baynard's Castle,' he told her, 'declared Northumberland a traitor, and the Princess Mary Queen.'

Jane sat down quickly. 'What a relief,' she said. 'I am very glad to hear it.' She smiled light-heartedly at Guilford. 'We are very glad to hear it.'

'From now', her father told her, 'you must content yourself with a private life.'

She nodded, and grinned happily up at him.

'Look. I . . .' Henry felt awkward. He had no words for what he wanted to tell her. 'Look, Jane. I ought to say . . .'

He tailed off, and Mrs Ellen spoke. 'The proverb says, a wonder lasts nine days, and then the puppy's eyes are open. So, what happens on the tenth day?' She was looking to Henry for the answer, but he did not have one.

Jane asked, 'Father, may we go home now?'

Henry looked from one woman to the other, and could not speak. He turned and made for the door.

Jane stood up and shouted after him, 'Father! May we go *home?*'

He stopped and slowly turned round. Haltingly he answered, 'I will . . . I will try to . . . to make amends.' With that he left the room abruptly.

Jane's face was anxious as she looked from Guilford to Mrs Ellen.

Within minutes Henry and Frances were hurrying away, with only a couple of attendants, across Tower Green. In the dawn light Henry glanced up at the flickeringly lit window of the Council Chamber.

The three of them sat on there, talking over what had

been and what would be, until the Lieutenant of the Tower entered, with guardsmen. He marched up to Jane, and did not bow. 'Jane Dudley?'

'Yes,' she replied.

'You must now come with me,' Bridges told her.

'Yes, yes,' she said, almost eagerly. She was not sure what was going on, but she knew that a crippling weight on her conscience had been removed. She looked down at the loose gown she wore. 'I will need to get some –'

'Indeed,' Bridges concurred. He turned briskly about and began to leave the chamber. Jane followed him.

Behind her she heard boots rasp on the floor, and a gasp from Guilford. She wheeled around, and in panic saw that the guardsmen had restrained Guilford from following her. 'No,' she shouted, 'No!'

She felt Bridges seize her elbow and tug her towards the door. The guardsmen, likewise, had now pinioned Guilford's arms to his side.

She shook her arm wildly, trying to free it. 'No, I will *not*. I refuse.'

One of the guardsmen detached himself and helped Bridges to drag Jane from the chamber.

'No!' her shout reached Guilford, as she disappeared. 'I will *not*.'

# IV

The Lieutenant of the Tower led Jane up the spiral staircase leading to the back of the royal apartments. Mrs Ellen followed. On a landing they met the housekeeper. Behind her were chambermaids with hessian bags, into which Jane could see her clothes had been stuffed, carelessly. The Marquess of Winchester was standing by, holding a long sheet of parchment.

'My Lord of Winchester,' Jane greeted him.

'My Lady,' the Lord Chancellor responded. He cleared his throat. 'I have had the task of pricking the inventory of items of which you have enjoyed the use during, ah, recent days.'

'I see.' Jane's voice was calmer, after her outburst in the Council Chamber. Once again she found her spirit had refreshed itself rapidly under duress.

Winchester was holding the sheet close to his nose to check it. The housekeeper, meanwhile, gestured toward the bags of clothes behind her. 'A number of items belonging to the royal household cannot be found among your personal belongings,' she told Jane.

'Can they not?' Jane answered, and held her arms above her head to prove that the items in question were not concealed about her person. 'Well,' she said sarcastically, 'as you see . . .' She shrugged, and fixed her gaze on the housekeeper, since they, and everyone else there, knew perfectly well what a ridiculous pantomime all this was.

But the housekeeper hardened her mouth and avoided Jane's eye, and Winchester began his inexorable recital. 'Three mufflers, one of sable, two of ermine. Two hats of purple velvet, set with pearls . . .' The old man's voice droned on, kirtles, bodices, stockings, shoes, until Jane could bear it no longer.

She rushed past the housekeeper and grabbed one of the hessian bags. As she pulled its contents out, she flung the garments at Winchester. A satin bodice wrapped itself about his knees, shoes and jewellery rattled on the stone stairs. 'Look,' Jane said angrily, 'these are my own things. Please take anything of them that you want. Please.'

Winchester's face was primly shocked, and the housekeeper's mouth was pursed in disapproval. Bridges was hovering in alarm. Only Mrs Ellen was self-possessed. As Jane stopped throwing clothes around, the old nurse stepped forward and picked up a pair of shoes. 'You will need these,' she remarked. 'Now we must be going on, your Grace.' She corrected herself. 'My Lady.'

Winchester came closer to Jane to tell her, softly, 'Her Majesty will be entering these rooms tomorrow, you see, ma'am. I am so sorry.'

Jane was mollified. She took the shoes from Mrs Ellen and put them on. While the nurse was quickly picking up the scattered garments, folding them neatly, and returning them to the bags the chambermaids would bring, Jane had a question she wanted to ask the Lord Chancellor. 'Please,' she said, 'would your Lordship ask Her Majesty . . .'

'Yes?' Winchester gave her a little smile. 'What is it?'

'When shall I see my husband?'

'Ah.' The smile faded on Winchester's face but, still sympathetic, he promised her, 'I will try for you, my Lady.'

'Thank you.'

Bridges led her out of the White Tower, across the Green, to a small keep in the outer walls. The cell in which he locked her was furnished simply, and lit by a barred window.

She sat on the bed, and looked at the small object she had all this time been gripping in her hand. It was the silver shilling, with her head on it. She was pleased that they had not taken that from her.

For days she could hear, through the little barred window, a distant noise of celebration. The church bells were rung incessantly, bonfires blazed, people danced in the streets and embraced each other, for joy that the Duke of Northumberland had been overthrown, and Queen Mary had come into her own.

In Cambridge, where Northumberland had accepted defeat, he tore down with his own hands the proclamation, in the marketplace, of Queen Jane's accession. He shouted 'Long live Queen Mary', and laughed, tears running down to the corners of his mouth. When arrested, he begged on his knees for mercy. Behind him his servants were running away, ripping the badge of the bear and ragged staff from their livery. He was escorted to London. The crowds would have pulled him down from his horse and lynched him if his guards had not used pike and halberd to protect him. The people contented themselves then with throwing stones and garbage at him. Through Bishopsgate, Shoreditch, the tumult was unparalleled. Stained with filth, bareheaded, he came to the Tower. Bridges put him in a cell with Gates and his son Robert Dudley. In the same keep Cranmer was sharing a cell with four other Protestant clergymen.

To the sound of trumpets and the pealing of belfries Queen Mary rode on a white horse across Tower Green to take up residence in the royal lodgings. Chief among the nobility accompanying her was the Earl of Arundel, who bore the sword of state. Cowled friars followed her in a procession. At the entrance to the White Tower she was met by Lieutenant Bridges at the head of a party of aged men, including the Duke of Norfolk and several Catholic priests, all richly dressed in the splendour of the olden days. They fell to their knees in front of Mary.

'These are my prisoners,' she declared. 'Honest men, incarcerated these years by those who appointed themselves my brother's ministers. But by the grace of God, and the name of His Son, Our Saviour Jesus Christ, they are prisoners no more.'

The men on their knees held their hands together, their faces raised, as they prayed and wept for joy.

'As no man shall be held prisoner', Mary continued, 'who with honest heart doth spurn all heresy, and confess with true religion.'

The Suffolks were among those who would not be held prisoners, for they had been allowed to return to their homes after expressing their penitence for the part they had played in delaying Mary's accession. In their humble submission they made no reference to their daughter Jane. She had embodied their hopes, and she had failed them. Let the Queen decide her fate.

Northumberland knew Queen Mary to be a merciful woman, and said so, aloud, when his companions needed encouragement. He developed the habit of crossing himself, and saying 'Kyrie Eleison'. After some days he had himself transferred to a smaller cell, where he could be alone, and on his table he asked for a crucifix to be placed, with some candles and a picture of Our Lady.

Guilford was allowed by Bridges to leave his own cell and go along the passage to visit his father. When he saw the display on the table he was shocked. 'You have betrayed me, Father,' he declared.

'How now?' Northumberland answered. 'Betrayed you, Guilford? Oh no.'

Guilford gestured to what he saw as the paraphernalia of superstition. 'You will put in peril your immortal soul.'

'Or save it, by Our Lady,' Northumberland replied, and crossed himself.

'For a few more years of miserable life.'

The Duke was not offended. Rather, his face wore a smile of wry amusement. He shrugged. 'Well, you know, it does not look so very miserable when you fear you are about to lose it. To be a living dog suddenly seems far more desirable than becoming a dead lion, as the wisdom of Ecclesiastes teaches us. So you may find.' He turned away from his son, and his voice was lowered. 'I wasn't very good at it, you see.'

'At what?'

'I misjudged men, Guilford. I misjudged you.'

'How so, father?'

'Do they let you see her?' the Duke asked.

'No.'

'Who would have thought it?' Northumberland was still turned away, shaking his head slowly. 'That the black sheep, that the most prodigal of all the prodigals, would find a love so simple, and . . . so pure. It puts us all to shame.'

Guilford thought he heard a sob in his father's voice. 'Father . . .' he started to say, but felt a thickness in his own throat.

When Northumberland faced his son, his eyes were brimming with tears. 'I did it for you all,' he said, and his hands made a little spreading gesture. 'Lands, properties . . . you were all to have them after me.' His voice rose. 'But they were not mine, you see. They belonged to God. I stole them.' He paused, mouth open with sincerity. He wanted Guilford to understand, and perhaps to forgive.

Guilford swallowed, and sniffed.

His father turned away again, so that the darkness of the cell shadowed his face. 'You see, what I believed was that a man, without the intercession of priest, or Pope, can look on God and say, Lord, here I am.' He nodded, and repeated, 'Here I am.' He paused, reflecting. 'But how may I look Him in the eye, when I can scarcely bear to turn my face to you, my son?'

Northumberland waited, perhaps for Guilford to speak, even to embrace him. Guilford could do neither thing. More than by the sombre circumstances, he was moved by his father's speaking to him man to man for the first time in his life.

Very quietly, the Duke asked, 'Why did you shame me, Guilford?'

Since none of the words in his heart would come to his mouth, Guilford turned and left.

A little while later Northumberland was kneeling in the small Catholic chapel of the prison, while the priest intoned a psalm. Guards watched.

Bridges arrived at the door, waited for the psalm to end, and then approached the Duke. 'My Lord.' He paused. 'I am sorry.'

With his hands still pressed together in supplication, Northumberland looked up at the Lieutenant. He thought for a time, and then said nothing but 'Well.' At his trial in Westminster Hall, newly furnished for the occasion, he had said all he could in his defence. He had acted constitutionally under the Great Seal, he told the presiding Duke of Norfolk, whom he had kept in prison for six years. And the Councillors and Lords gathered to try him, every one of them had put his signature to King Edward's will of succession. How could they pronounce him guilty? And now they had done so, and there was no reprieve. 'Well.'

'Sir John Gates will precede you to the block,' Bridges told him. 'Your elder sons have both been pardoned. As have the Duke of Suffolk and the Duchess. Her Majesty is anxious that her reign be not stained with much blood from the outset.'

'Yes,' Northumberland said. 'And Guilford?'

'I have not yet been informed.'

'I see. Am I permitted to hear Mass again, before . . . before the end?'

'Of course, my Lord.'

‘For this journey’, said Northumberland, ‘I will need the sustenance of Our Lord’s body.’

From the window of her cell Jane watched the procession cross the Green, heading for Tower Hill. Bridges led the way, followed by Northumberland and Gates, both elegantly dressed, and two priests in cassocks. Halberdiers surrounded them. Outside, thousands were waiting, beating drums, singing and dancing. The halberdiers would prevent the crowd from anticipating the headsman’s work, but afterwards there would be a great scramble to collect souvenirs, such as blood soaked up with a rag brought for the purpose.

Pray God, Jane thought, I do not die as they die, fallen miserably back among superstitious cant. When it is my time to die, pray God I have the courage to meet my Maker with dignity, alone.

She spent most of her hours at the window, and most of them wishing that she could see Guilford.

With a knock at the door of the cell, Mrs Ellen was admitted. She carried a note. ‘My Lady,’ she said, with a little excitement in her voice, ‘the Queen will see you.’

‘When, Mrs Ellen?’

‘Today, ma’am.’

Mary was waiting for her in the small state room where Jane had spent many hours during the nine days of her reign. It had been altered in one striking respect: hanging on a wall was a large portrait of Philip of Spain, son of the Emperor Charles V.

Jane curtsied. ‘I wrote a letter,’ she said.

‘Yes,’ Mary answered. ‘I read it.’

‘I was trying to explain that although I took upon me that of which I was not worthy, yet no one can ever say that I sought it, or that I was pleased with it –'

'I know,' Mary told her, 'I know. It was not your fault. Well, perhaps it did show a want of prudence. But you are very young.' She smiled at Jane. 'Are you receiving enough money for your needs? Are you eating well?'

'Through your Grace's goodness and mercy, yes, thank you. There is but one thing –'

'I'm pleased,' Mary interrupted her. She had something serious to tell her little cousin. 'You will both have to be tried, you know. It should not be for a few months yet, I think, when the people's heads will not be as hot as they are now. And naturally you will be condemned to death, for treason. But, as you know, I have the prerogative of reprieving, and I intend to use it, of course.'

Mixed with the relief Jane felt was a stab of fear that Mary might require her to embrace the old religion. She blurted out, 'Your Grace will impose no conditions?'

'Well,' Mary answered sharply, 'it would sound well were you to promise not to steal my throne again.'

Jane knew that she was properly rebuked for her impulsive question, and she quickly knelt before the Queen. 'Your Grace, what I have allowed to be done and imputed to me covers me now with the deepest guilt and shame, and all that I am able to do is throw myself upon your Grace's great clemency and –'

'Now, now,' Mary said, taking Jane by the arm and lifting her to her feet, 'that is enough of that. Come.' She walked across the room. 'I want to show you something.' She stood in front of the portrait, taking out her eyeglasses to examine it. 'Philip, Prince of Spain,' she told Jane. 'The son of the Holy Roman Emperor, Charles. The portrait was painted by a Signor Titian.

They tell me that I should view it from a distance. Unfortunately, from a distance I find things most difficult to view.'

Jane was not sure what was expected of her. 'It is . . . a good picture,' she said.

'Yes,' said the Queen.

'Is it a good likeness of His Highness?'

'I couldn't say,' Mary replied, and didn't say that she had fallen passionately in love with the young Habsburg's image. Once, many years ago, when she had been younger than Jane was now, her hand in marriage had been offered to the Prince's father, but Charles had refused it after hearing the lamentably small dowry that King Henry VIII had in mind. 'You married in the first flush of your youth,' Mary told Jane. 'You are lucky.' After studying the portrait a moment more, she put away her glasses. 'Now you must go,' she said. 'Ambassadors are waiting upon me.'

In her desperation to see Guilford, Jane succumbed again to an impulse, and blurted, 'Oh, Ma'am, forgive me, but there is one further mercy you could grant me –'

Sharply, Mary cut her off. 'Say nothing that will change my mind.' She took a breath, and more quietly added, 'You didn't heed my warning to take care, little cousin Jane.'

Jane curtsied, and turned to leave. At the doorway she passed Lady Anne Wharton, and heard her announce, 'Your Grace, his Excellency.'

The Spanish Ambassador, Renard, caught sight of Jane as he entered. Gracefully he crossed the room, knelt before the Queen, and kissed her hand. Lady Anne withdrew and closed the door.

'Your Excellency,' Mary greeted him, in the Spanish

she had spoken with her Aragonese mother, 'you are most welcome.'

'Your Grace,' Renard murmured. 'I am overwhelmed to see you at last in the place that belongs to you.'

'I am most grateful,' Mary told him, and continued in English. 'So, Excellency, what news do you bring us?'

Renard folded his hands. 'The Emperor is quite delighted by the fair prospect of his son being honoured with your hand, your Grace.'

'Then pray tell the Emperor that our delight in no way is exceeded by his.'

Renard nodded courteously, then more carefully enquired, 'Your Grace, may I ask, was that the young usurper I saw leaving your presence?'

'It was.'

Renard pursed his lips and stroked his beard with his fingers. 'I am bound to inform your Grace that the Emperor is *not* delighted that there should remain, within your realm –'

'No.' Mary stopped him firmly. 'We have already told your Excellency.' The previous time he had raised the question, Renard had learnedly cited the Emperor Theodosius as a precedent for the ruthless suppression of all potentially dangerous claimants to the throne, even among one's closest relations. 'No,' Mary repeated.

Mary kept her word. The trial was held over until the leaves had turned brown and fallen, and the people had started to forget about Queen Jane, who had never seemed to them more than a punctuation mark inserted in the royal succession by the Duke of Northumberland. Those months of late summer and autumn were happy ones for Jane, even in the confines of the prison, because Mary also kept a word she had not given: Guilford was allowed to share a cell with his wife. And she had books, paper and pens, and a supply of spiced biscuits. She pursued her studies and became still more fervidly attached to the reformed religion. As though seeking to provoke those in whose power she was, she grew more formidable in her tirades against Catholicism. Hearing that an old tutor of hers had returned to that faith, she said that she marvelled that one who had been 'the beautiful temple of God' had become 'the stinking and filthy kennel of Satan, the unshamefaced paramour of anti-Christ, thou white-livered milksop'.

On a chilly autumn morning, when the leaves were scurrying across Tower Green, Sir John Bridges called them out of their cell. Jane had dressed all in black, and she carried a Prayer Book to read as they went to the trial.

With Bridges and the prisoners, guarded by halberdiers, marched the headsman. His axe was held so that the blade faced away from Jane and Guilford.

All around Tower Green the procession was watched in silence by those who worked there: the servants, clerks, bakers, farriers, and the workers in the Royal Mint. In the streets on the way to the Guildhall it was the same, people watching in silence, pitying these two children who, after all, were simply victims of Northumberland, like many another. And some there were who thought that, all said and done, the little Jane might have made a better Queen than this Mary, who was going to take a Spaniard to her throne and bed.

In the Guildhall the Duke of Norfolk presided, flanked by Arundel and Winchester. The charge of treason was read out, the prisoners pleaded guilty, and Norfolk at once pronounced sentence. 'Jane Dudley. Guilford Dudley. You have been found guilty of high treason. The sentence of this court is that you, Jane Dudley, be beheaded in the precincts of the Tower and, Guilford Dudley, that you be taken from that place to Tower Hill, where your head shall also be struck from your body. And may Almighty God have mercy on your souls.'

While the Duke was speaking, the headsman had slowly revolved his axe so that the blade was facing the condemned. Both Jane's and Guilford's faces went white, even though they had heard no more than they expected, and knew that they could count on the Queen's clemency.

The blade of the axe faced them through their journey back to the cell. At first the procession was watched in silence again. But then a voice shouted, 'God save the Lady Jane!' The halberdiers wheeled around, to identify the culprit, but now the shout was taken up all around, 'God save the Lady Jane! Long live the Lady Jane!' Those who were not shouting clapped those who were, and everyone was eager to let Jane see a smile of sympathy and encouragement. The tumult grew so loud that Bridges was obliged simply to hasten the procession back to Tower Green and into the keeps as quickly as possible. Even a shout of 'Long live Queen Jane' had to be ignored.

'Did you hear that?' Jane asked Guilford, when they were alone. 'Did you hear those cheers, those shouts?' She no more desired the throne now than she ever had, but the common people's cries had shriven some of the guilt she felt, vindicated her innocence amid the evil that had been done.

'Yes.' Guilford had apparently taken no joy from it all. 'Yes, I heard them.'

'Don't you see?' Jane asked, trying to stir him from the morbidity into which she supposed the sentence had plunged him. 'She could not execute us *now*.'

'Oh, Jane.' Guilford looked at her ruefully.

'What?'

'It's you who do not see.'

She frowned, a little put out.

'Don't you know *why* they cheered you?' Guilford asked.

She shrugged. 'Well, because . . .' And in truth she could not think why. The common people always had been mysterious to her.

Guilford took her hand in his. 'The Queen has told the Commons that she intends to be married to Philip, Prince of Spain. A Spaniard – to be the King of England. Can you imagine how that has been received among the people? Can you? And moreover there is a young pretender to the throne, alive, already married, of the Tudor blood. Can you see why they were cheering you?'

She bit her lip. She understood now.

'So,' Guilford went on, 'if you have prayers to say, then pray that the Queen will change her mind. And pray that not a soul will cheer for you, darling Jane.'

After a pause, she remarked, 'Mary loves him.'

'Hmm?'

'She does, Guilford. I saw her looking at the portrait of him that she has.'

'Well?'

'And I saw me, looking up at you.'

Everyone knew that the Spaniards were outlandish strangers who, with Prince Philip as their foothold, would enslave the kingdom of England, and think it naught to ravish a man's wife before his face. In vain did priests in the pulpits promise their congregations that much wealth would accrue to needy England from the fabulous treasure that Spain had brought out of the New World. Nor did anyone believe the story, propagated by Ambassador Renard, that the opposition to Philip was fomented by the perfidious French, who were chagrined to see the alliance between England and Spain cemented. Rebellious factions were rising all over the country. Some declared that the Lady Elizabeth should ascend the throne, and others called for the return of the Lady Jane. A young man who said that he was Edward VI, not dead at all, made a brief appearance outside the Tower, and a longer one within it.

At Bradgate Manor, Henry Suffolk sat in a hallway, being booted and spurred by a servant. Someone had hastened to tell Frances, and now she swept in and stared, appalled, at her husband.

'You're mad,' she told him.

Henry eased his foot into a boot and answered, with deliberation, 'I am not mad.'

'Where are you going?'

Henry stood up. Clattering slowly into the courtyard, with Frances dogging him, he explained to her, in a sententious voice, 'I am going to Leicester. Sir Thomas Wyatt leads the force in Kent. Master Peter Carew is raising troops in Exeter. My men shall march from Leicester, then from Coventry.'

'Unto where?'

'London.'

Frances swallowed, and found it in herself to approach her husband meekly. She laid her hand on his arm. 'My love, don't go,' she asked. 'Leave well alone. We are alive. So England will marry Spain. So a crabbed and bitter woman will be made happy by it. And we – we are alive, Henry.'

It nearly worked. Henry paused, reflected. He remembered how he had felt, that night in the Council Chamber, tearing down the canopy, his stomach filled with fear that he might not have much longer to live. Then he remembered Jane's face that night, how happy she had been to hear that she was no longer required to be Queen of England. 'Father, may we go home now?' He turned to Frances. 'No.'

She spun away.

'I owe it to our daughter,' he said.

His wife's back was turned to him.

'She has need of me.' He waited, and Frances said nothing, and so he signalled to the servant and climbed onto his horse.

As he rode out of the courtyard Frances called after him, 'And will she thank you, Henry Grey?'

In the cell, Jane sat at the table, nibbling at a plate of food. Guilford was at the window. Outside, across the Green, soldiers with torches were rushing busily about.

'What is happening?' Jane asked.

'I cannot tell,' Guilford answered. 'There are so many

soldiers, I think it must mean that some of the rebel forces have reached London.'

'Why will no one tell us what goes on?' Jane complained.

Mrs Ellen came in to clear away the meal, and Jane greeted her eagerly. 'Mrs Ellen, tell us, what have you heard?'

As she stacked plates onto a tray the old nurse replied, 'What I have heard say is that the people from Devonshire have been halted. And the main force that is coming from the north is said to have got no further yet than Coventry.'

'And my father? What of him?'

Mrs Ellen lifted up the tray. 'I do not know, my Lady. All is rumour, in any case.' She had heard of the stoning of priests, of a dead dog, tonsured, hurled through the window of Queen Mary's bedchamber. Better not to speak of such things to her Lady Jane. She did not want the girl made anxious.

The night passed, and another day, and the next night still the voices were shouting commands outside the window, and the noise of boots marching did not abate.

Jane and Guilford were trying to play a game of chess, but she found it impossible to concentrate. Finally she pushed the pieces over on the board. 'I simply cannot bear the not knowing,' she said. 'It is intolerable.'

'We must be patient,' he told her.

'Why?'

'There is nothing we can do, in any case.'

'Yes there *is*. We can *know*. Knowing is doing, Guilford.'

He sighed. He did have a scrap of information that he thought better withheld from her, but now, feeling slightly abashed, he decided to impart it. 'I did hear the gaoler remark that he had seen fires burning over in Southwark.'

'And who lit them? And why?'

'I cannot say. I believe I also heard him muttering something about a duke who was riding from Warwickshire.'

'Oh Guilford,' she exclaimed, looking wide-eyed at him, 'this is madness.'

'No,' he said, picking up the chessmen, 'no, it's not. There is a logic in it.'

'What logic?'

Very well, Guilford thought bitterly, I will tell her how things truly stand, and she will make her own judgement of the case. 'It is your father,' he said.

Her mouth opened. 'What?'

'Yes. I know it for a fact.'

'My father? But . . . but what would my father be . . .'

'I will tell you, Jane. He is making amends. That is how he would put it, I'll be bound. Amends.' Guilford was smiling crookedly. The son of a villain had married the daughter of a fool, and what his father had nearly brought about would be accomplished by hers. A year ago, in the stews where those fires were now burning, he had known nothing. Now he knew much, and the fruit of it was sharp anger.

The next morning he felt a dull doom take hold of him when Sir John Bridges entered the cell, attended by Mrs Ellen, whose mouth was twitching nervously, and by two guards. Guilford tensed himself, to put on a brave face. 'Is there any news, Sir John?'

Bridges spoke slowly and precisely. 'Queen Mary

addressed the citizens last night, from the balcony at Guildhall.'

Jane regarded him with a perplexed face. 'So what?'

'It was a brave act, my Lady.' Bridges's hands were clenched at his sides. 'Your father had reached Ludgate.'

' "Had"?'

The Lieutenant cleared his throat. 'The Duke of Suffolk was arrested by the forces of the Queen's Majesty two hours ago. At Temple Bar. I am sorry, madam.'

Guilford blurted out the question that mattered. 'The rebels, who were they calling for?'

'I beg your pardon?' Bridges said.

'Come, Sir John, tell us, please. Were the rebel forces calling out in the name of any particular person?'

Bridges looked at Guilford and gave him his answer, in a dry voice. 'Aye, my Lord. They shouted for "Queen Jane".'

Guilford could hardly bear to look at Jane, but he had to. The colour had drained from her face, as she saw it had from his, too.

Kindly, Bridges told Guilford, 'My Lord, you must now accompany us, if you please.'

Jane was stuttering, 'But – why, again . . .'

'Because, ma'am,' the Lieutenant told her, 'it is not considered meet that you should remain any longer together, in these times.' He half turned his head to the guards, who at once seized Guilford and hustled him away.

Jane was stiff with panic. 'Guilford! Don't let them harm you! Say anything they want you to.'

★

No matter what it might cost her, or what the citizenry and the nobility might think of it, Queen Mary was determined to be married to her Spanish prince. She confided to Ambassador Renard, 'I consider myself to be His Highness's wife. I will never take another husband. I would rather lose my crown and my life.' If Arundel was to be believed, the Privy Council had indeed given serious thought to deposing her in favour of her sister Elizabeth. That alarmed her chiefly lest, in losing the crown, she lost much more. The Emperor Charles was marrying his son to the Queen of England, not to the Lady Mary.

Now here was Renard come with an ultimatum. His Highness was ready to set sail from Spain. He would do so, said Renard, 'the instant that he can be assured that there is no threat of further civil discord in your realm, Ma'am. Oh – let us not mince words – when there is no longer any *focus* for such discord. I refer, ma'am, to one now inhabiting this Tower.'

Mary, standing erect, was frowning, and the lines of her age were etched in the skin of her face. She glanced up at the portrait of Philip beneath which they were speaking.

Renard saw her hesitation, and made an irritable little snort. Firmly, as though reproving a wayward daughter, he said, 'Madam. I cannot put it any plainer. After the late events in this kingdom, if you want to marry His Highness, then Jane of Suffolk must go immediately to the death that, in your English law, she has fully deserved. And her husband must go with her, of course.'

And still the woman hesitated. He saw great pain on her face. What was he to do, then? – send for the prince and see him molested by this rabble of English citizens?

With a shrug close to despair, he played another card. 'It might be acceptable to His Imperial Majesty were Jane of Suffolk, and her husband, to be conveyed to a prison in Spain.'

He need not have bothered. She was gazing at the portrait, as though it might speak to her, tell her what she should do. Well, Renard reflected, His Highness had indeed just spoken to his betrothed, through the Embassy. There was nothing more to say.

'Your Grace,' he said, 'I am the message-bearer, no more. I cannot make terms with your Grace.'

Mary spoke. 'Tell me, your Excellency. We wonder if . . . Would these children be less a threat were they to embrace the true religion? Can you say?'

Her eyes were pleading with him. Renard shrugged and, trying not to sound too sceptical, grunted, 'Less.'

A fire was burning in the grate to keep the chill from Jane's cell. Seated beside the window, she looked out at a grey sky full of birds wheeling and gliding. Her eyes returned to the book on her lap. She was reading Plato again. She silently mouthed the words in English: The soul takes flight to the world that is invisible . . .' She smiled sadly, remembering that she had had to correct Guilford for his rendering it as 'unknowable'. One of the most touching things, during their time together in here, had been that Guilford enlisted himself as her pupil in Greek. For her part, she had learned to play chess with him.

She returned to the text: 'but there arriving, she is sure of bliss – and forever dwells in paradise.'

The door was opened, and Sir John Bridges entered. 'Madam, this is the Queen's Confessor.' He stood aside and Dr Feckenham came in. Behind him, accompanied by guards, was Guilford.

'Guilford!' Jane was on her feet and trying to run into his arms, but Bridges restrained her.

Guilford, also held by the guards, spoke urgently. 'Oh, Jane, they want us both –'

Sharply, but not unkindly, Feckenham cut him off. 'You promised to be silent, sir!'

Guilford bit his lip, and nodded.

'Why,' Jane said, smiling, 'it is you, Dr Feckenham.'

'So you remember me?' The priest was pleased, too.

Jane nodded toward Guilford. 'If I may not embrace my husband, why have you brought him here to me?'

Feckenham looked solemnly at her. 'To help you to resolve in your mind, my Lady, whether your next leaving of this room will be your last.'

Jane went white. Feckenham nodded to Bridges, who withdrew, taking the guards with him. Guilford remained standing by the door, which was locked.

'Madam,' Feckenham said to Jane, 'I lament your heavy case. Yet I doubt not that you bear this sorrow with fortitude and a patient mind.'

'You are most welcome, Dr Feckenham,' she replied, 'if you have come to offer me Christian exhortation.'

'Madam, I have come, I pray, to save your life, by convincing you to renounce your pernicious heresies.'

Jane hesitated, in surprise. 'Her Grace made a promise to me, that no conditions would be made.'

'That was before your father, alas, was leader of an insurrection in your name and pretended title.'

Jane made a small gesture with her hands. She understood.

'So,' Feckenham asked, 'will you talk with me?' He

motioned towards the chair, for her to sit.

Jane's eyes found Guilford's. From behind Feckenham's back, he shook his head.

Jane sat down. 'We shall waste our time,' she said. 'You are much deceived if you think that I have any desire of longer life. The time has become so odious to me that I long for death, and will willingly undergo it. Neither did I wish the Queen to be solicited for such a purpose.'

Feckenham nodded. 'How many are the sacraments?'

'There are two. The sacrament of baptism, and the sacrament of the last supper.'

'No, my Lady, there are seven. The sacraments of baptism, confirmation,' – he counted them on his fingers – 'the Eucharist, penance, Holy Orders, matrimony, and last unction.'

'Then tell me, Dr Feckenham, in what scriptures find you that?'

Feckenham, who had been leaning forward, sat back in his chair, and paused before continuing, 'Then tell me, how shall a Christian soul come to God?'

Jane's answers were starting to sound mechanical. 'By believing in His name, and by no other means.'

'What,' Feckenham asked, 'is nothing else at all to be required?'

'No, nothing at all, for as Paul writes, faith and faith only justifies.'

'Speak, I pray you, of the sacrament of the Eucharist. Do you not receive the blood and body of Our Lord?'

'No, I do not.'

'Did not Our Saviour say –'

Jane was becoming weary of it. 'Was He the vine? Was He – a door?' Her eyes were pleading with

Feckenham to allow an end to this charade.

He stood up. On his face was grief.

More softly, Jane said, 'Our disputation may be fit for the living, but not for the dying. Leave me to make my peace with God.'

'You are right, my Lady,' Feckenham acknowledged. 'And the Queen is wrong.'

'Is she so?'

Feckenham sighed. 'How may I – how could I – score across a faith so pure, and firm, and resolute? We are, indeed, wasting the time we spend on it.'

She looked at him, in great surprise.

'I am sorry for you,' Feckenham told her, with sincerity, 'for I am sure that we two shall never meet after our time on this earth is ended.'

'True it is,' she answered, 'except God turn your heart. For I am assured, unless you repent and turn to God, you are in evil case. I pray to Him, in the bowels of His mercy, that he send you His Holy Spirit to open the eyes of your heart, for He has given you His great gift of utterance.'

Feckenham looked at her, with infinite sadness in his eyes. 'I make you this promise, if you will allow it, that I will be with you to the end.'

He stood, and knocked at the door. Bridges opened it and let him out. Mrs Ellen was there.

Feckenham looked bleakly at them. 'I have – have done all that I can,' he said.

Bridges nodded. He was no less sad, having made of Jane a true friend, he told people. He whispered to a messenger, who ran off along the corridor.

In the cell Jane had stood up, and was leaning on the table. 'He is . . .' she said, 'he is in evil case.' Now that

Feckenham had left she could allow her feelings to show on her face. 'He will burn in hell,' she sobbed. 'His soul will burn for all eternity. He is a kind man, a good man, he wants to save me.' She turned her face to Guilford. Tears were running down her cheeks. 'And he will burn for ever.' Her voice rose with the agony of it. 'Can that be, Guilford? Oh, can that truly be?'

Guilford took her in his arms. 'Jane. Jane.'

'It *cannot* be, Guilford.' Her body was shaking wildly in his arms, as the sobbing overpowered her. 'It cannot be.'

'Jane,' Guilford said, 'listen. Please.'

'Yes. Yes, I am listening.'

'He came to me first. And this I know, that without the strength you have given me, I would never have been able to stay firm.'

'Stay firm? For what?'

Guilford frowned. How could she ask? 'For the sake of my immortal soul.'

'Oh, yes . . .'

'And for the sake of our nine days,' he added. 'To keep the memory of them untarnished. Unbetrayed.'

She looked up at him. 'They brought you here, having told you to be silent. Their hope was that I would believe that they had broken you. But they did not understand at all. Without you here with me, I would never have been able to remain true.'

'And so,' Guilford mused, 'without each other we –' The irony hit him. 'We would both still be alive at this hour tomorrow.'

Jane was calm now, and strong in her faith. 'Oh,' she replied, 'but we shall be.'

Guilford looked at her, terrible doubt on his face.

'We will have taken flight', she said, 'to the world that is invisible, where we are sure of bliss . . .'

He held her tightly now. 'And we will dwell in paradise,' he concluded.

The messenger came back to Bridges with a sealed document. The Lieutenant opened it and read it quickly. Then he turned to the guards. Before he could give them the order, he felt Dr Feckenham's hand on his arm.

'Please,' Feckenham asked very gently. 'For an hour.'

Bridges clenched his fingers anxiously. He did not know what to do.

Feckenham persuaded, 'Whatever may become of their souls, in the flesh they have but one night remaining to them.'

Bridges looked sideways at his guards. It was irregular.

'What harm?' Feckenham insisted. 'To leave them to each other, for the space of an hour?'

The Lieutenant surrendered. He nodded curtly to the guards, who withdrew a little way down the corridor.

The fire in the grate was dying, but its embers cast a glow over Jane and Guilford, who knelt before it, facing each other, their hands clasping each other's, as they recapitulated the little time they had had together.

'So, then, we will,' he said.

'Oh, yes,' Jane responded, 'we will.'

'We will fly.'

'We will fly.'

'Away, beyond their reach.'

'So far . . .'

'Their touch cannot tarnish us,' he said.

With one hand, he stroked her cheek tenderly, seeing

the glint of her eye as the shadows of his fingers moved over it.

'And at last,' he resumed, 'we will be –'

'Nothing,' she said.

'Nobody.'

'Each other's.'

They paused, their arms around each other. 'But this time,' Guilford whispered, close to her ear, 'for ever.'

The door burst open and suddenly the room was full of dark, armed men, Bridges at their head. Jane and Guilford instinctively snatched their clothes to their naked bodies. Mrs Ellen, following the guards, gasped.

'My Lady –' Bridges began.

Guilford was about to ask Bridges to leave them a few more minutes, at least for decency's sake, but Jane spoke before him, very gently. 'Let them be. The next time that I see your face, I want it for eternity.' She turned away, not looking at him any more.

Guilford hesitated, looked at her, and understood. He rose to his feet, pulling his shirt on, and walked to the door. There he paused for a moment, about to turn back to her, but did not do so. Instead he walked out of the cell.

Mrs Ellen was helping Jane to put on her under-dress. When that was done Jane went to stand by the window, looking down to the Green. Bridges gestured to the guards to leave the cell and followed them out, locking the door.

On the Green a noise of hammering had started. In a torchlit circle Jane could see carpenters building a scaffold.

★

She left the window and sat down at the table. The rest of the night she spent in writing. To her father, awaiting his own execution, she wrote:

Although it has pleased God to hasten my death by you, by whom my life should rather have been lengthened, yet can I so patiently take it that I yield God more hearty thanks for shortening my woeful days than if all the world had been given into my possession with life lengthened at my own will. My dear Father, if I may without offence rejoice in my own mishaps, herein I may account myself blessed, that, washing my hands with my innocence, my guiltless blood may cry before the Lord. To me there is nothing that can be more welcome than from this vale of misery to aspire to that heavenly throne of all joy and pleasure with Christ my Saviour. May the Lord continue to keep you, that at the last we may meet in Heaven with the Father, the Son and the Holy Ghost. Your obedient daughter till death.

Renard had already written a letter to Philip of Spain, assuring him that he could now come to meet his bride without fear of offence from the citizenry.

Jane wrote letters of farewell to her sisters, and to those who had taught her. Then she composed a prayer for herself.

I am Thy workmanship, created in Christ Jesus. Assuredly, as Thou canst, so Thou wilt, deliver me when it shall please Thee, for Thou knowest better what is good for me than I do. Therefore do with me in all things what Thou wilt. Only, in the meantime, arm me, I beseech Thee, that I may stand fast.

In the Chiltern Hills the little skiff she had found, and Guilford had rowed, was frozen solid in the stream.

In her Prayer Book, she wrote an inscription on the flyleaf.

> While God assists us, envy bites in vain.
> If God forsake us, fruitless all our pain.
> I hope for light after the darkness.

Finally she composed the words she wished to speak from the scaffold.

Winter sunlight streamed through the window in the morning. The shadow of the bars moved slowly across the wall. Jane had dressed in the black gown she had worn at her trial, with a black head-dress. She continued to sit at the table but had nothing more to write. Mrs Ellen and other ladies-in-waiting stood near the door.

Dr Feckenham was admitted. To Jane he said, 'I gave you my promise, and I repeat it. Up to the end.'

Jane's eyes closed and she turned her head away. 'Please,' she said to Feckenham, 'please tell me. I want to know.'

He sat down at the table, facing her, and spoke gently. 'Your husband was taken from his cell, by the Lieutenant of the Tower, through the Bulwark Gate. The sheriffs followed them, up to Tower Hill. There was a crowd, in whom I sensed much sympathy. He was led through them to the scaffold steps, just three of those.

He climbed them, he turned around, held the rail, and addressed the people, asking for God's forgiveness. And then he knelt, and said his prayers, in quite a clear voice. He rose from his knees, and embraced the gentlemen who were attending him. Then he took off his coat, his hat, and collar, and forgave the headsman, who bade him stand on the straw, before the block.'

Jane had not moved. Her face was impassive.

'He tied the handkerchief over his eyes himself and knelt, placing his head within the crevice of the block. When he was ready, he threw wide his arms, and the axe came down.'

Jane's nod of acknowledgement was barely perceptible.

'It was a single stroke,' Feckenham told her. 'He can have felt no pain. Nothing.'

'Nobody,' she whispered.

'My Lady?'

Jane shook her head. 'What happens now?' she asked. 'What happens to him?'

Neither Feckenham nor the women understood what she meant by the question.

'His body?' Jane asked.

'It is brought back to the precincts of the Tower,' Feckenham said, 'for Christian burial.'

She had stood up, quite suddenly, and now walked purposefully to the window, looking down at the Green, and particularly the entrance to the Chapel of St Peter Vincula. Birds wheeled in the sky.

Mrs Ellen and Dr Feckenham were both disconcerted.

'My Lady –' Mrs Ellen said.

'Madam,' Feckenham began, 'surely you do not –'

'No.' Jane shook her head at their alarm. 'My husband waits for me.'

Soon afterwards a cart was hauled across the Green, past the scaffold there and the small crowd that had gathered around it. In the cart was a body loosely wrapped in coarse cloth, stained with blood. Beside it was a smaller bundle, the cloth also stained dark.

Jane looked steadfastly down at Guilford's remains. It was what she had to do.

When the cart had been taken into the Chapel, she turned from the window. To the nurse and the priest, both watching her with concern she explained, 'You see, I love him.'

Feckenham nodded, slowly.

The door of the cell was opened. Sir John Bridges came in, and stood just inside. He said nothing.

Jane went to the table, picked up her Prayer Book, and waited. Feckenham made a little sign to the women and Bridges, who went outside and waited in the corridor. Feckenham joined them.

Jane put her arms about Mrs Ellen and embraced her comfortingly. Mrs Ellen started to cry. 'My Lady . . .'

'No, Mrs Ellen, no,' Jane told her gently, still with her arms about her. 'There is no need.'

She stood back. Then, holding the Prayer Book before her, she left the cell. Mrs Ellen followed her.

The crowd around the scaffold was not large. Only by permission could people attend an execution within the Tower. In the bitter, still morning air a thin cloud of breath hung about their heads, in the brightness of the sunlight.

All eyes were watching the White Tower when Jane came from it, a small figure among the officers, guards and yeomen warders before and behind her. As she walked across the Green she read to herself from her Prayer Book.

At the scaffold Bridges offered his hand to her as she mounted the three steps. Waiting at the top, representing the Queen, was the Earl of Arundel. Jane looked him in the eye. His eyes moved downwards.

She could not see the headsman, or the block. Everyone was so large, all around her, Bridges, Arundel, Feckenham, Mrs Ellen, guards, women. She had heard that the headsman was a huge, strong man, and would be dressed in scarlet, but she could not see him.

She asked Bridges, 'May I speak what is in my mind?'

'Yes, madam.'

She turned and clasped the rail of the scaffold. At least she could see now the people with their faces turned up to her.

'Good people,' she began, and was grateful to hear her voice steady and clear. 'I am come here to die for a crime which, though real, and grave, was not of my seeking, but of those who purportedly understand such things better than I. I pray you all to witness that I die a Christian woman, and I look to be saved by no other means than by mercy of my God, in the merit of the sacrifice of Jesus Christ, His only Son.'

There were those in the crowd who were moved to shout 'Shame!' and 'Let her live!' The halberdiers stationed at the periphery of the crowd gripped their pikes, and tried to see who was shouting.

Jane silenced them. 'And now, good people, while I am living, I beg you, pray for me.' There were no more shouts.

Jane looked nervously behind her, as though seeking reassurance that what she had performed so far was as it was supposed to be. She asked Feckenham, 'Shall I say this psalm?', and pointed to it in her Prayer Book.

He could not answer at once. He had to swallow and compose himself before, without looking at the Prayer Book, he answered, 'Yes, madam.'

She knelt down, facing the crowd, folded her hands in prayer, and recited the psalm from memory.

Have mercy upon me, O God, after Thy great goodness: according to the multitude of Thy mercies do away mine offences.

Kneeling beside her, Feckenham recited the psalm with her, in Latin: *Miserere mei, Deus . . .*
Against Thee only have I sinned, and done this evil in Thy sight: that Thou mightest be justified in Thy saying, and clear when Thou art judged.
Behold, I was shapen in wickedness: and in sin hath my mother conceived me.
But lo, Thou requirest truth in the inward parts: and shall make me to understand wisdom secretly . . .

When she had finished she stood up, and handed her Prayer Book to Bridges. 'You asked, sir, for a remembrance of me.'

Mrs Ellen and the other women took off her head-dress and her black gown, so that she stood in her under-dress, her neck open to the bitter air. From a sleeve of the gown she had taken a few small tokens, velvet ribbons and braiding strings, which she distributed to the women as she kissed them farewell. Mrs Ellen handed her a handkerchief.

She looked at Bridges, who turned, to guide her to the block. Then she hesitated and stepped across to face Dr Feckenham. 'God will requite you for your kindness, sir,' she told him. With a slight smile in her frightened eyes, she added, 'Though it was more unwelcome to me than my instant death is terrible.' To his astonishment, and perhaps to her own, she grasped his hand and stood on tiptoe to kiss him on the cheek. When he let go of her hand he found that she had passed something to him, a silver shilling with her head on it.

Quickly she turned and followed Bridges. The way had been cleared ahead of her, so that now, for the first time, she saw the block, surrounded by piles of straw, and beside it the huge figure of the headsman, dressed all in scarlet as she had been told.

The headsman bent one knee, and bowed his head. 'so you forgive me, madam?'

'Oh, willingly.'

The headsman stood up again. 'Please would you stand upon the straw,' he asked.

She complied, and began to bandage her eyes with the handkerchief. It was not easy to do, it slipped, and she saw the headsman offer to do it for her, but gestured him away.

When it was tied, she heard the headsman say, 'Now kneel, please, my Lady.'

She did so.

'And lay you down.' The headsman turned away and withdrew the axe from under the straw.

Jane had put her head down, as requested, but it was still on the straw. She had misjudged the distance to the block. Her hands reached out to feel for it. 'Where is it?' she asked, and still not finding it she became desperate. 'Where is it?'

The headsman was standing with the axe half-raised. The women's sobbing became shrill but no one moved. Everybody stared in horror at the tiny, blindfolded figure, hands pawing the air, scrabbling to reach the block.

'*What do I do?*' Jane's voice was panic-stricken.

Feckenham stepped forward. Glancing contemptuously at the headsman and at Bridges, who had attended so many executions, he took Jane's arm and guided her hands to find the block. Then he returned to his place.

He heard her say, 'Lord, into Thy hands I commend my spirit', and then the thud of the axe. He had closed his eyes. He heard a rustle of straw, a grunt from the headsman. Then the voice of the headsman, crying loudly across the Green, 'Behold the head of a traitor!'

Queen Mary held the shilling in her hand. Dr Feckenham had given it to her, because he did not need it as a remembrance.

They were standing together at the end of a long gallery at Greenwich Palace. A few yards away Renard stood at the head of a clutch of dignitaries, who were impatient to escort Her Majesty down to the river, where she would be introduced to Philip of Spain. But Mary was still anxious to have a complete account from

Feckenham of what he had seen at the Tower that morning.

'Did she die well?' Mary asked

'Yes, she did,' Feckenham answered. 'And now, your Grace . . .' He was as impatient as Renard for the Queen to leave. It disquieted him to find how much he resented her questions, and he would be glad when she ended the interview. Still she had not moved. 'Ma'am . . .?' Feckenham enquired.

Slowly Mary turned her head to look out of the window. At last he heard her murmur. 'I am going to meet my husband.' She turned back to her confessor, and in her voice was a note of desperation, of a woman at the extremities of what she could bear. As though it were something quaint, she explained, 'With whom – I am in love.' She peered at Feckenham. 'You see.'

Feckenham looked at her and could find nothing to say, although it seemed she expected some reply.

At a discreet cough from Renard she recovered herself. Handing the shilling back to Feckenham she set her shoulders, and walked towards the waiting dignitaries. With relief they formed themselves into the hierarchical order of attendance upon Her Majesty: Arundel, Winchester, Norfolk . . . Robert Dudley was in the procession, and so was Frances Grey.

A short woman, surrounded by tall men, Mary led her lords temporal and spiritual, knights and ladies, down the long gallery, with a painted ceiling and portraits on the walls.

The last in the procession was Feckenham. He paused to look out of a window and left the shilling on the sill. Outside, over the river, a flight of birds wheeled in the sky.

The procession disappeared at the far end of the gallery, but Feckenham stayed by the window. He needed a few minutes of solitude.

Watching the birds, he murmured to himself, 'The soul takes flight, to the world that is invisible . . . but there arriving, she is sure of bliss, and is released from the error and folly of humankind, their fears and their wild passions.' He watched the birds wheeling, backwards and forwards across the February sky, in patterns and purposes that he could not comprehend. 'And forever dwells in paradise,' he concluded.

# CASTLE CARNACK

A passionate romance on
the wild Cornish moors

Mary
Williams

When Sabrina, daughter of Sir Martin Penderrick, deserted her fiancé in the middle of their wedding, she expected the consequent uproar in the strict Edwardian society of the day. What she did not expect was her meeting with handsome Oliver Cavanagh, a rich businessman whose forbears had made a fortune from tea. Their unpredictable marriage sets off a pattern of dramatic events, leading to tragedy as well as passionate fulfilment . . .

**HISTORICAL ROMANCE 0 7221 9103 0 £1.95**